THE BENEFITS OF DEATH

When Mrs Leithan disappeared, her husband behaved very calmly and casually. He assured the police that she had gone away on a visit, and that there was nothing to worry about.

But the police were certain that Charles Leithan knew a lot more than he admitted, and they had good reasons: first there was a great deal of money involved; and second, his visits to his mistress became less furtive after his wife's disappearance.

Still more mysterious was the fact that her champion dog Stymie had disappeared at the same time. At last the police believe they have solved this mystery and despite the absence of a body a murder charge was brought before a jury . . .

THE BENEFITS
OF DEATH

Roderic Jeffries

First published 1963
by
William Collins, Sons & Co. Ltd.

This edition 2004 by BBC Audiobooks Ltd
published by arrangement with
the author

ISBN 0 7540 8655 0

British Library Cataloguing in Publication Data available

Printed and bound in Great Britain by
Antony Rowe Ltd., Chippenham, Wiltshire

CHAPTER I

CHARLES LEITHAN awoke and stared into the darkness. He wondered with irritation what the time was as the radiator to the right of the bed sounded a deep "clugg."

There was a wavering yowl from the far side of the garden and immediately the cry was repeated in a slightly higher key. The Cuencas were either panicking, swearing, or declaring inflamed passions: to Cuencas, all sounds were the same in the dark.

He climbed out of his bed and walked round the foot of the second, empty, bed to the south-facing window, the curtains of which he parted.

The night was heavily overcast so that he could see nothing outside but a small circle of light which moved slowly along the top of the slope. His first thoughts suggested poachers, but he discarded the idea. Poachers would be in the woods, and in any case, his land did not hold enough pheasants to attract anyone. With a sense of despair, he guessed that behind the torch was a policeman.

He went back to his bed, switched on the Italian-built, Empire style lamp whose wiring was always giving trouble, and dressed over his pyjamas.

He left the house by the back door, crossed the lawn and entered the field through the gateway beyond the western belt of ornamental trees. The Cuencas in the kennels heard him and yowled more loudly than ever.

As he shone the torch he carried, he was met by the beam of another torch and his head and shoulders were picked out in light.

"I'm sorry if we woke you," said a polite voice.

"What the hell are you doing here?" he demanded.

"Just looking around, sir."

"Where's your search warrant?"

"My what?"

"Search warrant."

The detective's voice suggested only slight amusement. "We didn't bother because we knew you wouldn't mind."

"It so happens I mind very much."

"You don't think that things are much better handled quietly?"

"You're not tramping all over my land in the middle of the night."

"Oh." The voice sounded vaguely disappointed. "We'll have to do the thing officially, then."

There was a silence. Leithan's mind became filled with a question that eventually he had to put. "What are you looking for?"

"Anything that'll help."

"And so you trespass? What would the chief constable say?"

"I've no idea, sir."

"He'd blast you to hell and back. The police haven't the powers."

"No."

"You woke me."

"Were you really sleeping?" The detective was surprised. "I suppose the dogs woke you? I've never heard a row quite like the one they make. Have you had their vocal chords doctored?"

"They're supposed to sound like that."

"Then I don't think I'd ever keep them."

"I'm very interested to hear it."

The detective ignored such elementary sarcasm. "I suppose we ought to be moving back to our beds. If the just don't get their sleep, they don't remain just."

"Why we?"

"My sergeant's down at the bottom of the slope.

Probably gazing into the stream to see what's crawling about in it. Although you'd never guess it to look at him, he's nuts about bugs. Etymologist, isn't it?"

Leithan allowed that to go uncorrected.

"Good night," said the detective, as he turned. He made it sound as if he had been paying a welcome courtesy call.

Leithan watched the light retreat until the rise of the ground abruptly hid it. He could, and should, have said so much, yet he had said so little.

He walked back towards the house and as he came abreast of the kennels the warbling yowls rose in volume. Suddenly, there were three sharp and piercing cries that suggested hysteria. That was Erymanthian who was on heat. Cuencas took nothing lightly, especially their sex life.

He shouted at the dogs to shut up and after a few muted protests they quieted. He went into the house and up to the bedroom. He stripped off the clothes over his pyjamas and thought about the letter of protest he'd write to the chief constable. As he climbed into bed, he knew no letter would ever be sent.

: :   : :

Seventy-four hours later, he was again awakened in the middle of the night by the dogs. He lay in his bed and listened to the noise as it grew in volume, suggesting that the cause of their alarm was closing on the kennels.

He tried to force his mind to consider his new book. Normally, once he had the plot, he found the actual writing easy, but for some time his mind had refused to act normally. Words would not form.

It was no good and at last he admitted it. He switched on the bedside light and at first it refused to work, but after a sharp struggle with the bar it did so.

He dressed and went downstairs into the garden and across the lawn. There was a light frost and the grass crackled under his feet. The gate, behind the red-leaved hedge of *Berberis Erecta Purpurea,* squeaked as he pushed it open: the dog-chorus increased. He looked round for the detectives and could not see them, so that when someone spoke close to him, he started.

"I'm sorry, we seem to have woken you again. Or perhaps you've been unable to sleep?"

"Why the bloody hell can't you do your searching in the day-time?" he demanded.

"We've so much work on our plates there just isn't time: I only wish we could spend our nights in bed."

"You're trying to panic me."

"Panic you, Mr. Leithan? Surely there's nothing we could panic you over?"

Leithan mentally cursed himself for his unhappy choice of words.

"By the way, did you write?" asked the detective.

"Write? Write to whom?"

"The chief constable. I'm rather interested to hear the answer."

Leithan suddenly flashed his torch upwards until its beam captured the other's face, but, almost inevitably, Jaeger merely looked interested.

Another man came up and spoke to the detective-inspector in a very low voice so that the words were no more than a mumble to Leithan. Jaeger nodded and then said: "It's cold enough to-night to freeze the brass monkey as well. D'you suppose there's any chance of a quick cup of something hot to keep the blood moving?"

If only to God, thought Leithan, he could refuse them, but they knew he would not because they might tell him a little of what he so desperately wanted to know. . . .

"I can manage something," he said angrily. He led the way to the house.

They went in by the second back door and along the short stretch of passage to the kitchen. Both Jaeger and the other man studied the fully equipped kitchen with open interest.

"You haven't met Detective-Sergeant Watters, have you, Mr. Leithan? My right-hand man."

Leithan nodded formally. Watters, in direct contrast to Jaeger, was large and rather shambling, and he looked as if his clothes were a little too big for his body and his skin was a little too big for his skeleton.

"It's a nice place you've got here," said Watters.

"We like it," replied Leithan, with emphasis on the "we." He plugged in the electric kettle.

"Not like the kitchen the force has landed me and the wife with. The only equipment's a gas stove that works when it feels like it and doesn't often feel like it."

"You're lucky to have that much," said Jaeger. "When I started, four bare walls were a luxury."

Leithan opened the sliding door of the cupboard above the double sink and brought down a tin of Nescafé, then went to the large refrigerator for a pint of milk—milk from his own herd of Jerseys with the cream thick on top and with plenty of taste because it was neither pasteurised nor homogenised.

"Have you lived here for very long?" asked Jaeger.

Leithan lined up three Cumbrian mugs. He tried to make out where the trap lay in the question. "Since we were married," he said finally.

"And when was that?"

"Thirteen years ago."

"Thirteen?"

For one wild moment, Leithan thought the other was going to refer to the unlucky number.

"Did you have to do much to the place?" Watters said. He leaned against one of the fitted cupboards with an easy casualness that suggested he always made himself completely at home.

"We carried out some alterations," replied Leithan.

Why bother to tell them that the builders had worked for nine months to remove the results of the previous owners' bad taste and to repair and renew where necessary.

The kettle boiled and the lid rattled up and down. Leithan mixed the coffee and then put sugar and milk, still in the bottle, on the table. His refusal to decant the milk was a mute gesture of antagonism.

Jaeger helped himself to sugar and milk. "You've no idea how good this is," he said, after the first two sips. "Very kind of you to ask us in."

"I took it to be a royal command."

Jaeger smiled and the expression removed the years from his face that his premature baldness added. "It's still good, whatever. You can't think how miserable the world becomes at three o'clock in the morning."

"The solution's simple. Stay in bed."

"D'you know, ever since I was a kid nothing has meant so much to me as my bed. When I retire, I'll make certain I never again spend a night away from it."

"You'll probably sign on somewhere as a night watchman, sir," said Watters cheerfully.

"Why d'you keep coming here in the middle of the night?" demanded Leithan. As soon as he had spoken, he wondered how he could have been so naïve.

Jaeger finished the coffee in his mug.

"At least you could carry on without stirring up the dogs," persisted Leithan clumsily.

"We don't do it deliberately," said Jaeger, in an injured tone of voice that was patently false.

Leithan noticed his right hand was shaking and he hastily put his mug down. Wasn't it Shakespeare who said that a shaking hand and sweating brow were the silent wraiths of guilt? He wanted a cigarette desperately and went to search in his coat pockets, only to find he was wearing a polo-neck sweater.

"Have one of these?" said Jaeger, as he took a packet of Oliviers from his mackintosh pocket.

Leithan picked out a cigarette with his left hand and was thankful that the hand was steady. One wraith that had been laid? He was about to search for a box of matches when Watters produced a gas lighter.

"What's the acreage of the place?" asked Jaeger.

"Eighty-three of arable and twenty-five of woods."

"Over a hundred, eh?"

"You've been over them all—you ought to know."

Jaeger gestured with his right hand and the cigarette smoke rose in a crested spiral.

"What are you searching for?" Despite all his efforts to do otherwise, Leithan still baldly blurted out the question.

"One never knows."

"You won't find anything."

"I hope not, sir."

"There's nothing to find."

"Then we'll certainly draw a blank, won't we?" Jaeger looked across at the kettle, from the spout of which steam was still rising. "Would it be straining hospitality too far, Mr. Leithan, to ask if there was another in the pot?"

Leithan waited while Watters finished his coffee, then he took their two mugs, washed them, and put in each a heaped teaspoonful of Nescafé. Faintly, from across the garden, he heard the yowling of the dogs.

CHAPTER II

I⊤ HAD BEEN a warm summer which lingered on through
September, so that even by the 1st of October the sky was
almost cloudless and the heat was such that light cotton
frocks could still be worn. Only the leaves of the trees,
turning into an exploding variety of browns, suggested
autumn.

The Cuenca club meeting was held on the lawns of
Lower Brakebourne Farm. Chairs and garden seats had
been set in a half circle, but none of these was occupied.
The guests had split into two groups, one of which stayed
behind the chairs and the other remained close to the
trestle table and the drinks. This latter group was
constantly filled with movement as hands reached out
and scooped up fresh glasses or refilled those they already
held.

The noise was considerable. There was the constant
rising and falling sound of human voices, but, far louder,
were the snuffles, growls, yowls, and hysterical shrieks,
of the dozen or so Cuencas.

Two men went round to the back of the trestle table
and met as each tried to pick up an unopened bottle of
whisky. "Sorry," said the first, but did not withdraw
his hand.

"Go ahead," said Leithan.

"Thanks, I will. Thirsty work, this, listening to so
much yapping. It's the first meeting I've been to and
it's a real eye-opener—or should I say ear-stopper?
D'you know something? If I thought anyone here had
a sense of humour, I'd explain to them why it's so
difficult to distinguish at first glance the humans from the

dogs. Look at the woman over there in the far group. Bulging eyes, pushed-in nose, and perpetually sniffing. Perfect example of the brachycephalic skull. And that one there, the fat one in the ghastly red dress . . ."

"My wife," said Leithan.

"Oh!" The man hesitated and desperately tried to find words to mend his gaffe. He looked quickly at Leithan's face, but the enigmatic expression he saw there failed to help him. Eventually, he decided to forgo his fourth whisky and returned to his wife who, lead in one hand and gin and bitters in the other, was describing in detail the sexual deficiencies of a bitch she had just bought.

Leithan gave himself another drink and wondered how Evadne would have been described, but for his interruption? Overshot? Apple headed? Not cryptorchidian, however. He found it very difficult to be able to picture her as she had been thirteen years ago when he had married her: perhaps the difficulty lay in his absolute belief that she must have been different.

A dog came round the back of the table. It sniffed his trousers and in its bulging eyes he seemed to detect the glimmering of a wish. He kicked it gently in the ribs to dissuade it. The dog left, bow-legs working furiously, shrill voice crying out.

He stared at the assembly. Short men and women, thin men and women, tall men and women, fat men and women. Some had dressed as though attending a garden party, others as if it had been only at the last moment that someone had told them that ties would be worn. In only one thing were they united. To drink as much of the free drink, and to smoke as many of the free cigarettes, as they possibly could.

He saw Alan Marsh approach and he tried to avoid the meeting, but was too late.

"Nice do," said Marsh. "Very nice do. Much

appreciated by one and all." His voice was heavy with the accents of his northern birthplace.

"Good," said Leithan.

"Proper decent of your wife, and no mistake."

"Don't forget, when you're handing out the bouquets, that I also, in my own small way, have contributed."

Marsh, who very seldom understood Leithan, fingered his lower lip with a gesture that he frequently used. "I was talking to Mrs. Cromby just now. Had a couple of gins, she had, and showing 'em." Marsh lowered his voice although there was no need to do this since the air was alive with the shrill cries of two bitches who were asking their owners to keep them apart in case they fought. "She says her and her husband'll come to the meeting providing their expenses are met."

"Expenses?"

"Aye. Evadne's idea, that was."

Leithan mentally recoiled from the use of his wife's Christian name by the other. It was said with such unctuous self-satisfaction.

"That's good news, eh?" demanded Marsh, eager for praise. He swept the palm of his right hand over his heavily greased hair. "What Mrs. Cromby says goes with her hubby, so that's two more in the kitty. You can tell Evadne, you can, there's no need to worry. Been a good fight, it has, but t'other side's lost. Couldn't match our strength, they couldn't. Take this party. Liquor 'em up and pretty soon they begin to feel they owe a debt for such friendliness. As I've always said in my business, put the other man under an obligation and you can't go wrong."

"D'you imagine Georgina is beginning to suffer a sense of obligation?"

"Our president?" Marsh guffawed shortly, as he looked quickly across the lawn at the far group of people and at the thin angular woman in the centre of it. "She

knows she's losing right enough. Mrs. Cromby told me
that she came up to her and said that self-interests must
be forgotten and that the only thing that mattered was
the good of the breed, which was why tri-colours mustn't
be allowed. Still—she wasn't to be persuaded, wasn't
our Mrs. Cromby."

"Perhaps Georgina Yerby forgot to offer expenses?"

"Hasn't enough brass to keep herself going proper,
she hasn't. No need to worry on that account."

Leithan had never found himself very much in
sympathy with Georgina Yerby; her personality was
cold; but just for the moment he was feeling very sorry
for her.

"Ah, well, very nice do your missus has given us all,
Charlie."

"Could you possibly make it Charles?"

Marsh helped himself to a king-sized gin and tonic.
"You don't like Charlie, do you? So sorry, but me and
the missus always talks of you as Charlie. Sounds warmer,
somehow."

Georgina Yerby walked into the clear space between
the two groups and said loudly, in her high, toneless
voice: "May I have your attention, please?" She was
thin, almost to the point of emaciation and it was obvious
that life had not treated her with too much generosity.
She dressed with care, if without taste, and the clothes
bore the obvious marks of heavy wear.

The sound of human voices ceased—only the canine
grunts, groans, yelps, yowls, and hysterical shrieks
remained.

"As some of you know, the annual general meeting of
the club will be held at two o'clock sharp on the 20th
of November at the Bambridge Rooms. One of the
subjects on the agenda will be the admission or rejection
of tri-colours in the breed standards."

Tri-colours were the 64,000 dollar question, and if

the battle was bloodless it was none the less bitter. The ordinary members of the club had never before been so aware of their importance: the president of the club tried to woo them and the vice-president tried to bribe them.

"To make certain you all understand the problem, I should like just to repeat the salient points. In the past, this breed has not advised the Kennel Club on the question of tri-colours within the breed standards and tri-colours have been allowed to be exhibited. Recently, because of the wish of certain members of this club, the question has been referred to the Kennel Club for a definitive ruling and they have held that the matter must be raised at our next annual general meeting where it is to be voted upon. The Kennel Club will accept whatever decision is reached. It is up to all members, therefore, as to whether or not tri-colour Cuencas are allowed to be entered in future shows."

"There should never have been any need for all this," said Evadne Leithan loudly.

Some of those who were present looked excited. They had hoped there would be trouble and this could well be the beginning of it.

Georgina Yerby's voice became higher. "If the records had been carefully consulted, perhaps it would not have occurred."

Evadne Leithan moved forward until she was directly facing the other woman. By comparison, she was a gross figure, but there was an air about her that said she didn't give a damn if she was fat, because the pearls round her neck and the two diamonds on her fingers were genuine. "The proper records were the ones that were destroyed in the Civil War. The trouble is that since then there've been a number of people over there in the breed who don't know what they're talking about when they say tri-colours aren't allowed. If only they'd

take the trouble to read *Murrell's Journal Of Spanish
Journeys* they'd discover that in the nineteenth century
he saw tri-coloured Cuencas which were then held to be
the most valuable and most esteemed of all dogs."

"Murrell also reported he saw a witch who rode her
broomstick across the roof-tops of Valencia," said
Georgina Yerby scornfully.

Leithan poured himself out another whisky. He prided
himself that he still maintained an equable neutrality
in the matter and therefore he found the affair petty and
degrading. So much energy, so much hate, so much deceit,
was being channelled into a project that wasn't worth a
tenth of the emotional effort. Georgina Yerby had,
together with her great friend who had died two years
before, started the Cuenca Club, fought its early battles,
and worked until the breed was recognised by the
Kennel Club who had granted one set of C.C.s a year.
Her bitch had won the first two challenge certificates—
the dogs failed to be awarded theirs—so that if it gained
the third one it would become a champion, the one
great goal in her life to which she was dedicated on
behalf of herself and her great friend.

At that time, Evadne had seen her first Cuenca and
had learned that a champion had yet to be made up.
She had determined to be the owner of that champion.
Stymphalian had cost two hundred guineas in Spain
and the transport and quarantine bills had come to
another hundred. Stymie won the next two challenge
certificates and the canine competitors were running
neck and neck. On the one hand a black and white
that was the second best Cuenca in England, on the other
a tri-colour that was the best. It was then that some of
the older members of the club, who knew what Georgina
Yerby had done for the club in the past and were bitter
about the use to which Evadne was putting her money,
had brought to the notice of the Kennel Club the fact

B

that tri-colours were barred in Spain and that they should, therefore, surely also be barred in England. If their request was accepted, not only would Evadne be prevented from owning the first champion, she would also be publicly labelled a fool for having paid two hundred guineas for a Cuenca that was incorrectly marked.

Leithan finished his drink. Evadne had taken up dog-showing and dog-breeding with a fervour that sometimes suggested she was trying to compensate for something. Was he in any way connected with that something?

He poured out another whisky as he listened to Evadne and Georgina Yerby continue their argument. The doctor had said on no account was Evadne to allow herself to become excited: the doctor had not known his patient.

: :   : :

Charles Leithan began work at ten in the morning and he continued at least until lunch. When all was going well, or he imagined it was, he did not finish until seven or eight at night. Evadne invariably jeered at him on such occasions, for wasting so much of his time.

As he sat down and pulled the movable table over the arms of the chair and removed the cover of the typewriter, he wondered if perhaps Evadne wasn't right. Sometimes the critics appreciated his latest book and reviewed it in reasonable terms, sometimes they disliked it and said so without too much spleen. In either case, the public remained distant. Not one of his books had ever sold more than three thousand copies on the home market, nor, even with subsidiary rights, had one ever made more than four hundred pounds. And that sum became rather ridiculous when compared with the income he and Evadne shared from the trust fund whose capital now stood at somewhere around a quarter of a million. Most people seemed to think his work was an apology for the fact that he did not have to earn a living, but that was one thing for which he would never apologise. He saw no evil in being wealthy and he wrote because he wanted to, perhaps even had to. The fact that the public received him in near silence upset him, but did not stop him: the fact that his wife thought him a fool to continue to scribble was of no account whatsoever.

He placed the two sheets of paper and the carbon in the typewriter and turned the roller until he could print 231 at the head of the page. Another thirty or forty pages and he would be finished. This time, he was certain he was writing a really good book, just as he was always certain. That certainty was in no way shaken by the knowledge that the future would prove he was wrong. If that seemed paradoxical, it was only a practical example of the way his mind worked.

He wrote stylised and somewhat sardonically flavoured novels which relied on characters and not action. Thirty years ago they might have been popular, but since then there had been too many changes in the world. He knew this.

He began to type.

: :   : :

The dining-room was in the more recently built part of the house, which was at right angles to the original. It was sufficiently large so that when there were only two of them eating there he often thought they must look slightly ridiculous. But Evadne would never agree to their eating any meal in the breakfast-room but breakfast.

"You're late," she said, as he entered.

He went to the chair at the far end of the refectory table and sat down. "I wanted to finish the chapter. Quite suddenly, I realised a way out of the trouble I'd got myself into."

She muttered impatiently and then helped herself to

four of the eight slices of smoked salmon. "I'm going up on the two-eighteen, Charles."

"Up where?"

She held a slice of lemon over the salmon. "I told you yesterday morning that I was going up to London."

"Oh, yes." He took the remaining smoked salmon and ground some pepper over the slices.

"Why don't you ever listen, Charles?"

"I usually do."

"You usually don't, so you'll kindly make the effort now. The new kennel-maid is coming this afternoon. I want you to explain her job to her and make quite certain she knows that Nemean is to have nothing but paunch until he's lost those extra pounds. She's to worm Ceryneian. I saw a segment in her big duties this morning." She began to eat. Evadne maintained her dogs on a rigid diet, but ignored the fact that she, also, was supposed to be on one.

Leithan filled his glass with water. "What time to-night are you coming back?"

"My dear Charles, I'm returning to-morrow, precisely as I've told you so many times already."

He tried to recollect what train she had mentioned, but failed.

"On the twelve o'clock," she snapped, clearly appreciating his difficulties. "I've told Mrs. Andrews that lunch will not be until one-thirty, but since her memory is nearly as bad as yours, you'd better remind her of that. I shall take the Rover and garage it at Crouch's for the night and tell them to have it waiting for the train." About to eat another mouthful of salmon, she looked across the table. "Have you written to the railway company complaining about that bridge?"

"Yes," he lied.

"They've no right to make their passengers go up and down so many steps."

"With a line between the platform and the car park, it would be difficult to have the thing level."

"That remark is just about up to standard."

Morosely, he watched her liberally butter a piece of brown bread.

"Marsh says that wretched woman from Hampstead won't agree to . . ." She stopped. "You're not listening. What are you thinking about?"

He was not prepared to explain he had been thinking of Pamela.

CHAPTER III

LEITHAN WATCHED his wife alter the setting of the safety belt until it would fit her ample measurements. She clipped the buckle into the holding catch and started the engine. "Look after yourself," he said automatically. "Have you got your pills?"

"Do stop fussing," she snapped. She confused illness with weakness and hated to be reminded that she suffered from *angina pectoris*.

"I'll take the new kennel-maid round and show her the routine," said Leithan.

"And tell her to worm Ceryneian." She pushed the selection lever to reverse. "Are you going out to-night, Charles?"

He shrugged his shoulders. "I may go to Lympne for a drink at the club if I feel like it."

She stared at him for a few seconds, then accelerated and reversed out of the garage. Leithan watched her round the U-shaped bend until she could turn right and drive down to the road. He wondered why she had bothered to ask him about his movements that evening? Until a few weeks ago, he would have said that their marriage had reached a reasonable state of co-existence, but recently he had twice discovered her looking through his desk—on each occasion she had claimed to be searching for something she must have known was not there—and whenever she went away for the night she asked him what he intended doing. When she came back, she was equally interested in what he had done.

One of the Ashford taxis came up the drive. Leithan walked round and met it in front of the house. The driver smiled and half saluted, then opened the back door. A woman climbed out and stared at Leithan. "I'm Sarah Pochard," she said, in a harsh voice.

He acknowledged her greeting. "If you'd take the bags . . ." he began to say to the driver.

"Very good, sir. I'll drop them in the front room—door's open, I suppose?"

Leithan nodded. Kennel-maids came and kennel-maids went—although the duties were light and the pay good Evadne could never be called the easiest of employers—and this driver knew the routine. Leithan gave him a ten-shilling tip and received in return a quick smile of thanks. The car drove off to cover the quarter of a mile between Lower Brakebourne Farm and the semi-detached house where the kennel-maid would live.

"Nice place you've got," said Sarah Pochard, almost resentfully. She scratched the back of her neck. "A thing I want to know is, what about hops?"

"There are always dances in Ashford and usually at least one a week in the local village hut."

"I'm telling you, I've had a basinful of village do's, I have. Too many clodding squares who want to show me what the other side of the hay-stack looks like."

Studying her heavy make-up, her prominently defined figure, and the sensuous set of her thick mouth, Leithan decided that in her twenty-four years she had seen the other sides of many hay-stacks.

"Your wife said as I'd have the use of a car?"

"We've a small van which you'll be using to collect the dog food from the slaughterhouse. When it's not wanted elsewhere, you're at liberty to use that. Within reason, of course."

She looked as if about to complain at the imposed restriction.

"Shall we have a quick look round the kennels so that I can explain what we'd like you to do?"

"If you say." She did not try to suggest that she was eager to begin work.

They walked past the garage and along the outside cinder path to the kennels. The Cuencas, all of whom had come into the outside pens, began to yowl.

Leithan stopped by the first pen. "We feed them twice a day. . . ."

"I know. She told me all that when I came for me interview. Ugly, ain't they?"

He thought it politic to veil his thoughts on the subject. "We keep these six out here and most of the time the seventh is in the house with us. Did Mrs. Leithan tell you their names?"

"No." She looked across the field to the south and saw the valley and the woods beyond. Her expression became still more sullen.

"Starting up there is Nemean: he's the only dog and he's at stud to approved bitches." Evadne charged a fifty guinea stud-fee to prevent the "erks and narks" from bettering their stock. "The others are all bitches. Going in order, Lernaean, Ceryneian, Erymanthian, Hippolyte, and Cerberus. Stymphalian is the bitch we have in the house."

"Gawd!" she said.

"Will you worm Ceryneian for a tape this afternoon. You'll find the pills in the tack room which is at the far end of the kennels. Make certain you only give one. Cuencas have very delicate stomachs."

"I'll bet."

"I believe Mrs. Leithan discussed with you the hours of work and all that sort of thing?"

"Yes."

"And you know where you'll be living?"

"That place up the road."

"Good. Let me know if there's anything you want."

She watched him walk away. Bloody snooty as they come, she thought, inaccurately. She went up to the nearest run and Nemean began a bubbling yowl and his eyes seemed to bulge more than ever. She stared at him with dislike. "You ugly bastard," she muttered.

: :   : :

Leithan drove in the Rapier to the Ashford/Ham Street road and then, just before Shap Cross, turned off and made his way through the narrow country lanes to Pamela's house. He wondered if all men of forty-two could slough twenty years just by taking a car ride. Perhaps not. They hadn't all a Pam waiting for them.

Her converted oast-house, with newly painted cowl on top of the roundel, had as a setting the wood that lay immediately behind it: it was difficult to believe there could ever have been one without the other.

Pamela opened the front door. She was wearing tartan trousers and a green shirt; there was a large smudge on her right cheek and her hair was in casual disorder. She smiled at him, and the happiness that smile gave him seemed momentarily to tie a knot in his stomach. She stood on one side so that he could enter, then she closed the door and immediately reached up and pulled his head down until she could kiss him.

She finally drew away. "So the headmistress is away for the day?"

"And the night."

"Well?"

He grinned. "So I thought you and me could have a little fun together."

They went through to the living-room which was circular, being the lower floor of the roundel. He noticed, with amusement, that as usual the room appeared to be in chaos with books, magazines, newspapers, a typewriter, and several box files, all in haphazard confusion. It was a far, and to him welcome, cry from the clinical neatness that always existed in his own house.

She picked up two books from the seat of the nearer arm-chair and dropped them on to the floor. As soon as he sat down, she curled up on his lap. "It's been absolutely months, Charles."

"Ten days since I was last here."

"Haven't you a spark of romance in you, you bastard?" she said affectionately. "I was suggesting it had seemed like months, but you . . . you know it's only been ten days and in any case they've only seemed like two to you. I'm damned if I know why I have anything to do with you."

"It's my fatal fattraction."

"Spare me such modesty. Don't forget something. Before I took you in hand, you were the most painfully pedantic and didactic man I'd ever met."

"Before you took me in hand, you hadn't met me."

"I can't think how any woman puts up with you." The moment she had said that, she knew it had been a mistake. She kissed him and soon the unfortunate reference was not even a memory.

Later, she went through to the kitchen to make some coffee and he followed her. "How's the work going?" he said.

"I wondered if you'd ever ask. Guess what?"

"With you, it could be anything."

"I've sold my latest book in America and the advance

comes to two hundred and seventy-eight pounds, four shillings and twopence, less agent's fees." She passed the coffee-grinder to him. "And if it sells at all, they've promised to take the previous three. Ever since I got the letter I've been trying to decide whether mink will suit me better than sable."

He turned the handle of the coffee-grinder a few times before he said: "Would you let me resolve the difficulty?"

"No, I wouldn't, and you damn' well know it. I'm willing and eager to commit adultery, but I'm not going to be paid for it."

"Pam, I didn't . . ."

"I know, you lovable old fool. You don't mean it like that and I'm all sorts of a swine for suggesting you did. Shall I let you into a secret? Sometimes, I get a lot of fun out of teasing you. You can be so very solemn, just like you were before I met you—and to save you telling me I couldn't know, other people told me. You realise, don't you, that when I was informed I'd meet a fellow author at the cocktail party it nearly put me right off it? 'A nice man, but just a little serious.' And when I was introduced to you, you said: 'How d'you do?' Exactly as if you'd feel hopelessly compromised by anything more. My first impulse was to empty a jug of water over you."

"Shall I tell you what the first thing I wanted to do was?"

"I've no desire to be reminded of the disgusting way you leered at me."

"Then I wasn't quite that pedantic?"

"You leered at me in a pedantic way. Get on with the coffee, Charles."

Later, they left the house and drove to Rye. Rye, with its pebbled streets that came from a different age, held a special significance for them. Their first meeting after the cocktail party had been there: a meeting she had tried to avoid even when she wanted it to take place. He might have been pedantic in some ways, but there had occurred between them that strange flash of spirit which accurately foretold the future. And although she continued to fight against their friendship for some time, because after the death of her husband she had sworn never again to become so deeply attached to any person that she could be mentally injured by that person, she had lost.

After dinner, they drove down to the sea, beyond Camber. They sat in the car and enjoyed the esoteric pleasure of seemingly being the only persons in the world.

On their return to her house he brought the car to a halt immediately outside the front gate. "O.K.?" he asked.

"Charles, must we . . ." She stopped, then opened the door. "All right."

He watched her climb out of the car and slam the door shut and he knew exactly what she had been about to say. But he could not leave the car all night in the front of the house in case it was recognised.

He drove on and turned right at the first cross-roads, then right again. This brought him to a track in the woods which eventually came to a natural clearing. He parked the car, locked the doors, and left.

He flashed the torch ahead of him and carefully stepped over the fallen elm. After four minutes, he came out at the back of the oast-house. She was in the sitting-room, drinking whisky, and it was immediately obvious that the storm warnings were flying. He was not surprised. They had been in sight for some time. He sighed.

"The drinks are over there," she said. She pointed at three bottles which were balanced on top of a pile of four thick books that were, in turn, on the window-sill. He poured himself out a stiff gin and vermouth and wished to God life didn't have to be so complicated. "Cheers."

She gave no answer, but finished her drink and handed him the glass for a refill.

He offered her a cigarette and when he flicked open his lighter, she suddenly said in a tight voice: "What are we going to do?"

He drank. "Do?" he queried. He knew his delaying tactics were completely futile, yet he still tried to delay.

"I can't go on like this." With a nervous gesture, she smoothed down the front of her frock into which she had changed before they went out.

He sat down on the gaudy pouf that her husband had brought back from Port Said. Strangely, he often thought of her husband as if he had been an old friend. "It's difficult . . ."

"Don't give me all the old stories, Charles. I know only too well that all the money's in a trust fund and that because your father had a ridiculous phobia about divorce you stand to lose everything if you're divorced. But so what?"

He lit his own cigarette. Did one really dismiss a quarter of a million pounds so casually?

She drank quickly. "Suppose she finds out about us and divorces you? Between us, we make enough to live on. It won't be the kind of luxury you're used to, but is that so very important?"

"I don't make a living, Pam, you know that. Six hundred a year, all told."

"And d'you know why it's so little? It's because you're isolated from the world, insulated by a fortune. You could write if you really had to. You could write damn' good books, much better than I could ever dream about, but because you're removed from life the stuff you turn out is dead. Didn't Mills say he reckoned you could easily become a first-class writer?"

"Yes, but . . ."

"If you were shot of all the trust money, you'd have to improve."

"And just suppose I didn't? What if you and Mills are wrong and that whatever I did I continued to limp along on six hundred? Then what?"

"Why suppose the worst? In any case, in a reasonable year I knock back fifteen hundred. Doesn't that make you want to stir yourself? I don't write because there's something inside me that's clamouring to come out: I write solely because when Bernard died my total assets were seven hundred and fifty quid. The stuff I churn out is muck, but I get paid for it because I know what kind of muck people like to read. For God's sake, Charles, don't go wasting yourself. Climb out of your ivory tower and dip your feet in the dung of the world so that you can experience its stink."

He finished his drink and then gave himself another. How did you explain the dread that accompanied money, the dread of losing its security? She was asking him to blindfold himself and jump into a pit full of serpents. If his writing wasn't any good at the moment, who could say what it might, or might not, become?

"What are you thinking?" she demanded. Her expression was hard and she looked her thirty-three years.

He returned to the pouf and sat down. "We agreed at the beginning . . ."

"We've been having a hole in the wall affair for just over two years," she said furiously. "For two years you've come and slept with me if and when that bloody bitch lets you off the string. Maybe you don't mind continuing that way, but I do. I want to have a family. Or hasn't that word ever occurred to you? Maybe you think of me as your cut-price prostitute?"

"Don't talk like that. I love you, more than anything."

"Not more than the money."

"It isn't that simple."

"You won't let it be. Study things in their true light and they all become rather sordid, don't they?"

"There's nothing sordid about us."

She finished her drink. "Give me another."

He hesitated.

"Are you worried about my getting too tight to perform?" she demanded.

He refilled her glass.

"You've got to make your mind up, Charles."

He handed her the glass and then stood by the side of her chair and rested his hand on her shoulder. "I know it's difficult for you, but . . ."

"Just forget the buts and start deciding. I need and want you desperately and there's nothing on God's earth I desire more than to have you with me all the time—but that doesn't mean I'm willing to put up with things as they are."

He withdrew his hand and went back to the pouf. Illogically, he was angry because she had spoken as she had. She had known the exact position from the beginning of their affair. He had kept nothing back, hidden nothing.

"You understand, don't you?" she said. "We're not going on like this. I just can't stand you leaving the car in the woods because you daren't put it in front of the house. I love you so very, very much," she said quietly.

Quite suddenly, the years began to leave her and she looked young and fresh. Her curved mouth seemed about to smile and her slightly turned-up nose derisively challenged the world.

: :   : :

He left her house at six and returned through the woods to his car. He felt, for the first time, as if he were engaged on something nasty and that made him furious. He and Evadne were poles apart so where was the wrong in enjoying the love of Pamela? There was no question of religious scruples because he did not even confess to the comforting religious beliefs of the average conforming Englishman, and he admitted only logic. But even logic seemed to have deserted him.

He reached the main road along which he continued until just before Kingsnorth. Then he entered the country lanes with their timeless turnings that he liked so much—although many of these lanes were ruined by a rash of bungalows and houses that disfigured the land as if it were suffering from an outbreak of acne. It was said that, because no one really cared, soon the whole of Kent would be little better than a dormitory town with the air black from the belching funnels of industry: when that happened, he would move and try to find somewhere where man did not strangle his environment.

He reached his house and drove into the garage. The dogs yowled a welcome and he distinguished the extra frenzy of Stymphalian. She was always completely outraged that he should so betray the deep friendship between them as to leave her in the kennels.

He let Stymie out of her pen and the other dogs watched in impotent fury. He stared at them with distaste and remembered the writer who had classified a Cuenca as the illegitimate offspring of a mange-ridden Griffon and a fractured Pekinese.

He went into the house and, inevitably, was struck by the clinical neatness everywhere and the contrast so formed with the place he had just left. The one was a home, the other wasn't. He went up to the bedroom and, after pulling back the cover, he sat on it to crumple the bedclothes. The first time he had told Pamela about his attempts to persuade Mrs. Andrews he had spent the night as he should have done, Pam had laughed. She would not laugh now.

He wondered what in the hell he was to do? Was it so

wrong not to want to view life outside the cover of the trust fund? What man, after enjoying an income that was close to ten thousand a year, would willingly take up life at six hundred? Pam believed that life without the umbrella would sharpen his writing and turn it into something good. But was she right? What if she were wrong and at the same time she found it less easy to sell her own work? Their combined income could dwindle until it was on the point of vanishing.

He fondled Stymie's ears. If he refused to break with the money, he would lose Pamela. But he daren't lose her. Equally, he daren't lose the money.

He suddenly thought of Evadne and in his imagination she had a jeering smile on her face.

The specialist had said that she could live for years if she took care of herself. Why, he thought bitterly?

CHAPTER IV

LEITHAN WALKED across the field to the concrete yard and the milking parlour beyond. The herd of Jerseys was a hobby of his, as was the whole farm, but both showed a profit. That was because he was deeply interested in them and because Ted Deakin was a born cowman who was careless about the hours he worked.

Deakin was swilling down the floor of the milking parlour. He saw Leithan and nodded his head quickly and then carried on with the job. He turned off the hose and used a squeegee to push the last of the water down the drain. His right arm had been badly injured in the war and three operations had left it an inch shorter than his other arm, but the physical handicap never seemed to hinder him.

He leaned on the end of the handle. "Milk's holding well, considering, and they're fair tearing into the silage. Sent off eighteen gallon more this week than last."

"How's Judy?"

"Bagging up nicely and if it ain't a heifer what's due, I'll keep pigs."

Leithan smiled. "Why?"

"She's heavy in the middle. Heavy in the back and it's a bull."

"Maybe! I was talking to an expert the other day about breeding and he said A.I. was giving better fertility results every time."

"Aye. There's some twist the facts round to suit 'emselves."

And that, thought Leithan, was that. Deakin considered A.I. was death to a good herd—indeed, almost the product of the devil—and insisted on keeping two bulls. Nothing would ever make him change his mind. "Is there anything you want in Ashford? I'm just on my way."

"The missus was talking about how she might be goin' in."

"I'll call in and see if she'd like a lift."

Deakin nodded his head. Then he said casually: "Alf's down in the ten-acre field putting up that new fence."

Leithan waited for a torrent of criticism.

"Not a bad worker, even if 'e looks at the watch a trifle close at times."

Leithan was surprised—and grateful. Deakin was the most intolerant of men when it came to his assistants. The previous one had lasted only three weeks before he fled Deakin's caustic tongue. "By the way, are you O.K. for cake?"

"The millers left a ton yesterday—said as the order

c

was overlooked, or something. I told 'em straight, overlook anything more and we was off. They ain't the only millers."

"I'll call into the cottage to see if Mrs. Deakin wants a lift."

Leithan went up the cinder path to the semi-detached cottages. As he came abreast of the right-hand one, he saw Sarah Pochard in the kitchen. She was making a cup of tea and when she looked out and saw him, a defiant expression crossed her face. She was not going to be with them very long, he thought.

Mrs. Deakin, an angular woman who ruled her household in a very old-fashioned way so that her two children still paid open respect towards their parents, accepted the lift into Ashford with alacrity.

Leithan walked to the garage and then drove back to Deakin's cottage in the Rapier. On arrival in Ashford, he dropped Mrs. Deakin outside the Odeon, after which he continued on to Parade Street where he was surprised to find he could park within sight of Enty's offices.

The girl at the reception desk on the ground floor smiled and said she was certain Mr. Enty would have time to see him and would he mind waiting just for a few moments? He went into the waiting-room and half-heartedly looked through one or two of the ancient copies of *Punch*. Finally, he sat down and studied the estate agent's advertisement of a forthcoming farm sale which was pasted up on the far wall.

Phillimore Enty was his half cousin. Their common ancestor was a grandfather whose escapades with a chorus girl had been responsible for the terms of the trust fund Leithan's father had drawn up. Leithan was never quite certain how this fact affected Enty and himself in terms of friendship. The difficulty of evaluating the answer was to try to decide how friendly they would have been had they not been related, and that was like telling a visitor he should have seen the roses the week before.

The receptionist came and said that Mr. Enty was free. Leithan went up the winding staircase to the first landing and then along to the far room. Enty was waiting in the doorway. "Hallo, Charles, how's the world treating you?" His voice was loud, almost booming.

"Not too badly."

"Come in and give me all the latest. How's Evadne? Or more important, I suppose, how is that herd of smelly dogs? Did you see the Schipperke on the telly the other evening? It tried to bite Dangerfield's finger and that, I thought, was bloody funny." Enty went round his desk and sat down in the swivel chair. He offered cigarettes. As always, he was dressed in a country check that was a trifle too flamboyant for the air of sober respectability most country solicitors deemed so essential.

They spoke for a few moments about family matters, then Leithan said: "I want a word about the trust."

Enty sprawled back in his chair. "Nothing wrong, I trust? Excuse me, quite unintentional, I assure you."

Leithan stared at the pile of law books on the far end of the desk. "I want to break it, Phil."

Enty blew out two smoke rings that chased each other across the room. "Yes?"

"I must break it."

"That's something of a tall order, Charles, as well you ought to know. Your father put the pistol to the heads of his solicitors and he saw to it that they gave him just what he wanted. The thing's tied up tighter than a banker's heart."

"It can't be impossible. The law's always got a dozen different faces."

Enty tipped back his chair until he could rest his knees on the edge of the desk. "You remember you asked me about this a couple of years back and I had a close look into it? We even got counsel's opinion because you were so insistent."

"I know all that."

"Counsel said that even if the trust was an odd one, under the existing law there'd be no hope of breaking it. In fact, some of the more stuffy judges would positively exalt it as promoting the sanctity of marriage. The divorce courts of this country do two things superlatively well—they breed perjury and sanctimoniousness."

Leithan became impatient with the other's apparent flippancy. "I haven't said anything about breaking up my marriage."

"No." Enty's voice became deliberately neutral, as if he suddenly realised that this was a professional and not a friendly visit. "I'm afraid, Charles, that when our mutual grandfather left your grandmother and went off with mine, he was unknowingly tying a very tight knot about you. In some ways, your father was rather too much of a moralist."

"That came from remembering how much my grandmother suffered."

"In order to avoid a family row in our generation, I won't argue on that one!" Enty's attitude always half suggested that he, also, would have gone off with the chorus girl. "The harsh fact is, Charles, that your father not only disliked our side of the family sufficiently much always to refer to us as bastards—I usually carry my birth certificate around for proof to the contrary—he was also determined that you should never have the chance to frolic off with a chorus girl. Consequently, the money remains in trust for you and Evadne until the death of either of you when the capital goes to the survivor and his or her children. In the event of a divorce, the money vests absolutely in the innocent party."

Leithan stubbed out his cigarette. "I want another opinion."

"You'll be wasting your money. The chap we had last time was the leading bloke on the subject."

"I don't give a damn. Try someone else. No one's infallible."

Enty scraped the ash from his cigarette into the ash-tray. "It's your money and why should I dissuade you too heartily when my profits depend on your generosity?"

"The trust talks about the guilty party. What happens if the two sides are held equally guilty?"

"There, my dear Charles, you have the kind of situation that ensures good digestions to us solicitors for years. Dammit, the litigation could be almost endless." Enty stroked the bushy moustache that seemed to broaden his already broad and rather fleshy face.

Leithan was aware that his present anger was quite illogical—he had known all the answers before he had put the questions.

Enty looked at his wrist-watch, a large gold one, with thick gold straps. "My throat never lets me down. It's drink time. Come and have a couple and a bite at the club?"

"Thanks, but Evadne's coming back from Town for lunch."

"There must at least be time for a drink?"

"All right."

Enty grinned amiably. "I'll just tell myself that that was said with wild enthusiasm. You know, old man, you may be thinking in terms of the trust as a real cow, but don't forget the size of the fortune." He stood up. "I don't mind saying that if my father had had half the business sense of yours, I'd burn joss-sticks to his memory no matter what the terms of the trust. Just think what I'd get my golf handicap down to!"

Leithan wondered what easy solution the other would have given to his present conflict of interests?

: :   : :

Evadne Leithan arrived home in a bad temper and this was not improved when she cross-examined Sarah Pochard and discovered that Nemean had not been wormed. Illogically, she rudely blamed the kennel-maid for not carrying out an order and then her husband for forgetting to give the order. Leithan retired to the study on the pretext of work.

During tea, when he had reluctantly joined her in the sitting-room, she said abruptly: "Did you go to the club last night?"

Leithan added sugar to his tea. "No, I didn't."

"You said you were going to."

"I changed my mind in the end. I was afraid I might meet Jim."

"Did you go out, then?"

"I went out in the car and had a couple of pints down in the Marsh at the Black Bull."

She cut herself a thick slice of the chocolate cream cake she had bought at Fortnum and Mason. Her thick and unsightly fingers lifted the cake on to her plate and the large solitaire diamond flashed ice-cold blues as her wrist turned. "Did you go on your own?"

"I hardly had time to import the chorus from The Windmill."

She ate a mouthful of cake and her jaws chomped up and down. Irresistibly, he was reminded of a Cuenca eating. As if that were Stymie's cue, the dog snuffled across to a couple of crumbs on the floor and licked them up.

"You might have taken that Breslow woman out."

He stared at her in shocked surprise. "Why pick on her?"

"You're friendly with her, aren't you?"

"Well, yes."

"Whenever you meet her at a cocktail party, you two always seem to huddle in a corner and have the world to talk about."

"That's natural. We both write."

"She surely doesn't flatter you enough to call your stuff 'writing'?"

"She thinks I'm reasonably good," he said stiffly.

"She's a slut." She finished the cake and then gave herself another large slice. On the floor, Stymie waited with bulging eyes for more crumbs.

"She's nothing of the sort," he snapped, unable to remain silent.

"They say she entertains half the males of the district and that if they don't leave something larger than a fiver on the mantelpiece, there's a hell of a row."

"That's a bloody lie."

"How would you know?"

He drank some tea and wondered bitterly what thoughts were tearing round in his wife's mind?

"Did you see her at all?" she persisted.

"No. Why should I have done?"

"Never know." She ate more cake. "The Marshes are fools."

He eagerly accepted the change of subject. "What's happened?"

"They tried to buy the Prestons' vote whereas if they'd an ounce of common sense between them they'd have known the Prestons live inside Georgina's pockets." She finished the cake, hesitated, and then with deep satisfaction cut herself a third slice.

"Well?"

"The Prestons are going to report to Georgina."

"I said it was a damnfool thing to do: you can't go around bribing people."

"Don't get in a panic. Marsh had just sufficient wit

to insist the money would only be for expenses and so Georgina won't be able to prove anything if she tries to take it to the Kennel Club."

"At least it will have put her on her guard."

"And small good that'll do her since she's as poor as a church mouse. And if she says anything to smear my name I'll have her up in court and she knows that. She's a fool—she won't admit she's beaten. We've over half the members promised to our side now, and there's still some to come. There are a couple in Yorkshire, those poisonous people we met at Crufts; Marsh reckons he'll be able to persuade them down." She finished her cake and put the plate on the table. "I've been thinking. Georgina isn't really the right kind of person to have as president of the club." She looked across at him.

"Don't forget she and her friend started it."

"That doesn't mean she's fit to be president. You can't have someone who daren't put her hand to a cheque book."

"Or are you determined to knock her out of the way because she's been brave enough to stand up against you?"

"You've no right to say that." Evadne's voice rose. "I'm only interested in one thing and that's the good of the club. Why d'you think I'm fighting for the retention of tri-colours?"

"To make Stymie the first champion. You don't give a solitary damn about the good of the club."

"You . . . how dare you say that." Her face became heavily flushed. "You like believing the very worst about me. You go out of your way to misrepresent me. You never worry about my feelings, never."

He was silent.

She put her right hand to her neck and tried to give the impression she was finding it difficult to breathe. "You know the specialist said I wasn't to be excited, but you go out of your way to excite me, don't you? I think you want me to have another attack."

"I think chocolate layer cake is likely to be more effective." He stood up and as he stepped clear of the seat his shoe accidentally brushed Stymie. She yowled so piteously that she might have been disembowelled.

"You swine," shouted Evadne, "trying to take your temper out on the dog." She bent down and took hold of Stymie and when the latter showed signs of wanting to go to Leithan, she dragged it backwards by its tail. "Poor little Stymie," she crooned. "Did he kick you hard because he was in such a terrible temper? Has the poor little doggie been injured and shall we send for the vet? Come on Mummy's lap and have a piece of cakie." She cut a large slice of cake and put it on her plate which she then took back from the table. She gave Stymie one twentieth of the slice and the remaining nineteen twentieths she ate herself.

Leithan walked to the door.

"You don't worry about me, do you?" she shouted.

He left the room. He could faintly hear her talking to Stymie, heaping endearments on the dog's head. Yet they both knew whom the dog would always prefer to be with, if only given the chance.

He went into the hall and tried to shed some of his anger. The old part of the house had been built somewhere between 1550 and 1600, and it had the typical sloping roof that, on the south side, came down to within six feet of the ground; originally, this had provided the outshut under which the animals had been tethered. Because of this slope, the hall was triangular in shape, with the right angle against the inside wall; this was fifteen feet high and timbered with beams that were black with age and pierced by myriads of woodworm holes. Between the beams, on specially made hooks that were carefully set in the original plaster of lime, sand, bullocks'

hair, cow-dung, and road scrapings, hung his collection
of old revolvers and pistols. He stared at them and
remembered some of the fun he had had in collecting
them. Because he had been a wealthy man, he had set
himself a limit of twenty-five pounds for any one piece.
Twenty years ago, it had been relatively easy to buy
good examples for that price, but now the experts would
be quick to say it was impossible. Nevertheless, he still
occasionally managed it.

He went out of the front door, paradoxically at the
back of the house, and stared across the garden at the
low brown-leaved beech hedge, the sloping field on which
some of the Jerseys were slowly making towards the
milking parlour, and the far woods. It was not a view of
distance, but to him it had immense depth. It was a
quintessence of the English countryside.

He looked to the south, and his mind flashed past
Shadoxhurst and fetched up at the woods before Shap
Cross. He wondered what Pam was doing at that
moment? Writing answers to the letters of the frustrated,
curious, or frantic readers of the women's magazines?
She worked on a freelance basis. When she had begun
the job and he had read some of the letters, he had laughed
at the writers: but very soon he had been upset by the
multitude of tragedies there were in life.

::   ::

Sarah Pochard quickly discovered that Cuencas were
smelly, snappy, fussy, adenoidal, delicate, and psychotic,
and that infection of their anal glands was their most
common complaint. She wondered what had made her
leave her last kennels, where they had kept Borzois and
Salukis.

She was no more enamoured of her employers than
she was of their dogs. Leithan worried her because she
was never certain whether he meant what he was saying:
Mrs. Leithan worried her because Mrs. Leithan was a

human bitch. Sarah's mother had been a bitch and she
was well up on the breed.

She began to cut up the paunch and tried not to smell
it. It beat her that in a home where money obviously
had no meaning, they should feed such muck. Green and
slimy, it was enough to upset a delicate young woman's
stomach for life. Respectable people fed their dogs on
dried meat.

When she had finished, she began to apportion the cut
paunch into the plastic bowls, but almost immediately
a lot of the pieces fell on to the floor. Cursing fluently,
she picked them up.

The dogs were yowling because they were hungry
and one of them—she didn't try to remember any of
their ridiculous names—sounded hysterical. In a fit of
temper, she went into the passageway between the sleeping compartments and the runs. "Shut your bleeding
mouths," she shouted, and she kicked the wire mesh of
the first door. Nemean's bulging eyes gazed at her with
frantic hate.

She went back to the tack room and collected the bowls
of food, then put one bowl in each compartment except
the third one, empty because they kept that dog in the
house.

She left the kennels and slowly walked in the field
towards her cottage in which, incredibly, there was no
television. When she was abreast of the garden, she
heard the Leithans talking and she stopped to listen.
She realised, with pleasure, that they were having a row.

"You saw her the day before yesterday."

"I've already said I didn't."

"You lied. You did see her. I know you did, because
your car was parked outside her house."

"And some kind neighbour rushed to tell you?"

"Do you admit it?"

"All right. I went over and saw her in the afternoon."

You're stupid, thought Sarah Pochard scornfully. Fancy admitting it. Now the old bitch would really go to town!

"Why did you lie?"

"For goodness' sake, quieten down, Evadne. You don't want them to hear you in Ashford."

"I don't care who hears. In any case, Ashford already knows. You've turned me into a laughing stock. Whenever I go away, you run straight to your little whore."

"She isn't."

Not much, thought Sarah Pochard.

"You've tried to make a fool out of me, Charles, but it's you who's the fool. I'll divorce you, and you know what'll happen then."

"You haven't any cause to divorce me."

"No cause! That's amusing. I've cause enough and you'll lose all your money; you won't get a penny from the trust. And it won't be any good coming to me because I shan't give you anything. You'll have to go begging to her and see what she'll give you."

More than you can, thought Sarah Pochard.

"I'm not going to keep on being treated like this. Why d'you keep seeing her?"

"I thought you'd already reached a firm conclusion on that point."

"I'm your wife, not her. What's she offering you that I can't?"

How stupid can you get, wondered Sarah Pochard?

"We discuss books."

This time, Evadne Leithan's comments matched the hidden listener's thoughts. "What d'you take me for? She ought to be on the streets of London."

"Shut up."

"I know my rights and I'm going to have 'em. Don't make any mistake there. If you want to run after that tart, you'll just have to keep on running." There was a harsh laugh. "You won't think it's quite so worth-while when you haven't got a penny to your name. You don't think you'll count for anything when you're poor, do you? You won't know what's hit you. You'll fold up and collapse because you haven't an ounce of backbone. D'you hear me, you'll collapse."

"Stop getting so excited."

"You'll be chucked out of this farm. You've thought about that, haven't you? The farm, the house, and the cars, all belong to the trust. So what about your precious cows? I'll send them all to the knacker's yard, I'll chuck salt over the grass you're always talking about, I'll rip out all the trees you've planted."

"You're mad."

"Let's see what you call me when everything's mine. Let's see how proud you are when you're begging me to take you back. What will you call me and what will you call your whore?"

"For the last time, she isn't my mistress and never has been."

"I'll get proof. Don't flatter yourself on that score. You're not nearly as clever as you think, and I'm not the fool you'd like me to be."

"What the hell's the use of explaining?"

"That's right, go away to bury your head in the sands. You're a complete failure, Charles, but because of your father's money you've never had to realise it. Now, you're going to learn. You won't keep her on the money you make from your scribbling."

Sarah Pochard's main thought became one of surprised interest. She was astonished to discover that Leithan had the courage to have a mistress.

CHAPTER V

LEITHAN PACED the floor of the study. The house had belonged to him—the trust—for only thirteen years, yet it had come to mean as much to him as if it had been in the family's possession for centuries. Now, he was threatened with its loss.

Surely he could live without being wealthy? His writing would improve as Pam always swore it would, and he would make enough money to maintain the two of them and the family that she longed for. He saw himself working with a new vigour and urgency, producing work that really mattered and that therefore people wanted to read. Then, the pendulum swung in the opposite direction and he visualised his editor, at the best of times humourless and lugubrious, shaking his head and saying that the state of fiction was getting even worse, that commercial libraries were now things of the past, that hardly any bookshops were left, and therefore, although the latest MS. was good, it would very regretfully have to be rejected. . . . Leithan suddenly suffered the absolute certainty that his writing wasn't any good. It was the hobby of a man who did not know what it was to have to earn a living. In a panicky manner, he tried to imagine what he would do if his writing failed him. What business or industry would take on a man of forty-two who possessed no qualifications beyond an M.A. obtained in the dim and distant past? Journalism? He was hardly made for the cut and thrust of that life. Farming? There was a world of difference between hobby farming, even if it did pay, and farming for a living. And where would he get the capital? With a sense of terrible isolation, he knew he dare not face the challenge. If that made him a coward, he was a coward.

But he had to face the challenge . . . unless he was ready to lose Pamela. Could he suffer such loss when she meant everything to him? Would he ever dare to leave Evadne and the trust fund?

He lit a cigarette. The agony of making a decision which he dare not make. What in the name of hell could he do?

: :   : :

The November fog covered much of Kent, and Lympne and Lydd airports were temporarily closed; the train services were running late, and all the roads south of Farningham were potential death traps.

Belinda and William O'Connell, driving from New Romney to London, gave the fog best at Kingsnorth. They stopped and were about to turn back for home when Belinda suggested calling in to see the Leithans. William O'Connell said that was a darned good idea, since the Leithans' daily woman could cook to some tune and Charles had a wine cellar that fairly made one's mouth water. The O'Connells had three children to educate and thus were seldom able to enjoy the pleasures of expensive living.

They left the Ashford road and, after one or two wrong turnings because of the fog, they reached Lower Brakebourne Farm. As her husband stopped the car, Belinda said: "I hope Evadne doesn't throw five fits at us turning up."

"She'll get over it," he replied, with the easy conscience of a man who had never suddenly had to provide a meal for two extra people.

They left the car and walked round the house to the front door (O'Connell, an accountant, was always annoyed that it was at the back), and as he rang the bell they heard the bubbling yowls of the dogs. "God knows why they keep those repulsive animals," he said.

"You're going the right way about being sent home with neither food nor drink," replied his wife. "You ought to know by now that the way to Evadne's heart is through her most beautiful dogs."

He made a rude comment.

Mrs. Andrews opened the door and smiled as she recognised them.

"We're stranded travellers," said Belinda.

"'T'ain't right for man nor beast to be around in this weather. Come on in and I'll tell Mr. Leithan you're here." Mrs. Andrews did everything quickly, including speaking.

They went into the sitting-room and Belinda looked round at the writing-desk without stands, the carved oak corner cupboard and settle table, the very ornate square Chinese lacquered cabinet, the Dutch gable bookcase which housed a small collection of Jacobite snuff-boxes, and the modern conservatively styled armchairs, all of which lived in harmony with one another and the overhead shaped oak beams and the large inglenook fireplace. She also studied the thick pile of the fitted carpet, the hand-painted lampshades on the wrought-iron standard lamps, and the hand-painted French curtains, and felt pure envy for anyone who could live amongst such beauty.

Leithan came in.

"Sorry and all that," said O'Connell, with little sign of apology in his voice, "but we're stranded travellers and Belinda said she was certain you wouldn't object too much if we dropped in."

"*I* said it?" protested his wife.

"Certainly. I'd never have the nerve to interrupt a famous author at his work."

Leithan smiled. "Now I know who's lying. Have a drink?"

"Isn't Evadne in?" asked Belinda.

"She went up to London earlier on. It's the annual general meeting of the Cuenca Club in a couple of days and she's got some organising to do."

"I hope she gets there in this fog. We wondered about train-ing it, but decided not."

Leithan asked them what they would have to drink and then poured out Cinzano for Belinda and himself and a whisky for O'Connell.

"Here's cheers," said Leithan, as he raised his glass.

They drank. "You look as if you've been on the tiles for weeks," said O'Connell breezily. "Life's one long dissipation."

"The work isn't going too well," answered Leithan shortly.

"You call it work? I wish you could have my job for a week just to discover what the word really means."

"Presumably, sitting in someone else's chair, drinking his drink?"

Belinda smiled. "You asked for that," she said to her husband.

Mrs. Andrews came into the room and said she had taken two steaks from the deep freeze and how did the visitors like them? Leithan observed dryly that he was glad to hear he had guests for luncheon.

O'Connell drank more than his share of the two bottles of Château Cheval Blanc and as a consequence his laughter was loud and frequent, and he told three stories that almost brought a blush to his wife's cheeks. When they had finished eating, they went through to the sitting-room for coffee.

"How about a liqueur?" asked Leithan.

"Bill's had quite enough," said Belinda. "He's

D

smiling with his eyes shut and that's always a bad
sign."

"Nonsense," retorted O'Connell, "you're just wilfully
misinterpreting the visible enjoyment of a gastronome.
I'll have a very large cognac, Charles."

"You're a pig," she said.

Leithan went through to the dining-room and returned
with a bottle of Otard and three glasses. "You'd better
hang on here until the fog clears."

"Thanks," replied Belinda, "but if we're not going to
London, there's a mound of work to do at home and
once we've digested the marvellous meal and I think
Bill's fit to drive, we'll battle back."

O'Connell was about to protest when the telephone
rang. Leithan went into the hall, leaving the door open
behind him. He picked up the receiver. "Hallo."

"Is that you, Charles?"

"Yes." He was annoyed by people who did not say
who they were, but in the present instance there was no
mistaking the soapy, northern accents of Alan Marsh.

"Charles, Evadne wasn't on the train. Judy had
prepared a special meal and bought a right lovely Dover
sole for Evadne."

"She caught the right train, but it'll have been late
because of the fog."

"You don't understand. We didn't want her to have
to struggle with luggage and such like, so me and Judy
drove to Charing Cross. Her train weren't no more than
fifteen minutes late, but she weren't on it."

"She must have been."

"I keep telling you, she weren't. I even bought a
platform ticket to help carry the luggage."

"Then she . . ."

"When people had finished getting off, I went along
looking to see if she were waiting in one of the compartments. She weren't there."

"She may have got by you without your seeing her, even though she had Stymie."

"Judy stayed at the barrier. Where is she?"

"How the devil should I know?"

"You must do."

"I dropped her at the station to catch the 11.42."

"But she wasn't on it when it arrived. We waited for the next one and she wasn't on that either, so we drove back here, and she isn't here. Hadn't we better tell someone?"

"Don't be ridiculous."

There was a pause. "Why not?" said Marsh.

"She can't be missing."

"But she wasn't on the train."

"It stopped all along the line because it's Sunday; she may have got off at one of the intervening stations."

"Are you sure we shouldn't tell someone?"

"Use some common sense."

"All right." Another, and longer pause. "She will be at the A.G.M., won't she?"

"For God's sake, why shouldn't she be?"

"I . . . I don't know. Are you coming up?"

"Yes."

"It was a lovely Dover sole. Judy bought just the one, specially for her, and now it's spoiled."

"I'll read the memorial service," said Leithan harshly.

"I . . . I'll let you know when she comes, Charlie." Marsh rang off.

Leithan replaced the telephone receiver. He took a handkerchief from his pocket and wiped his brow as he stared through the window at the fog. From the right, came the dimmed sounds of the dogs.

He returned to the sitting-room and was immediately aware of the regard the other two gave him. "Evadne is going to stay with some people in Town and hasn't turned up on the train she was going to catch."

"Then she can't have caught it," said Belinda, with a down-to-earth practicality. "Presumably, you didn't actually see her on to it at this end?"

"Didn't what?"

"See her on to the train at Ashford station?"

Leithan shook his head. "I was going to, but she told me not to stop and fuss round her."

"I'm sure she'll be all right," said O'Connell uneasily. "Nothing can have happened to her."

"No," said Leithan, "nothing." He brushed back a stray hair that had curled over his forehead. "What about the cognac?" He poured out the three drinks and handed the glasses round. He drank quickly.

"That's the first time I've ever seen you treat such precious liquid so cavalierly," said O'Connell, in an ill-advised attempt to lighten the atmosphere.

Leithan offered cigarettes. He lit his own and could not conceal the fact that his right hand was shaking.

Mrs. Andrews knocked on the door—a formality, since Leithan had left it open, but she worshipped formalities —and carried in the large square silver salver on which were black basalt cups and saucers, Queen Anne silver coffee-pot, and milk jug. She had a reverence for the trappings of luxury and never missed an opportunity of producing them. "Did you enjoy lunch?" she asked anxiously. "I'm sorry I didn't have no time to do anything proper."

"It was excellent," Belinda assured her. "There isn't anyone between here and the coast who can cook like you do."

Mrs. Andrews beamed with pleasure and retired from the room. Not for the first time, she wished that her husband, who laboured on the railway, had a quarter of the taste of the people of Lower Brakebourne Farm. She was a complete snob, and very proud of the fact.

Leithan poured himself out another drink.

"We must be off very soon," said Belinda. She gave her husband a look which said that he had better agree.

Ten minutes later, the O'Connells left and began their slow drive home. Leithan returned to the sitting-room and poured himself out his third cognac. He drank it, lit a cigarette, and then as he heard Mrs. Andrews approach he hurriedly made his way into the study through the doorway between the two rooms—a reminder of the days when the outshut had been beyond.

He looked down at his typewriter. For days, he had not written a word that was worthwhile, which was why he had been trying to work on a Sunday. But to continue the attempt would be ridiculous and he decided to go for a walk.

He heard a yowling and was certain it was Stymie. He drew in his breath sharply, then hurried through to the hall. Forgetting the need of a coat, he ran into the garden and called out "Stymie." The cold, damp atmosphere, a striking contrast with the centrally heated air inside, made him shiver.

The world lay under an unnatural silence as the fog, lifting slowly, rendered both men and animals almost immobile.

"Stymie," he shouted. The dogs in the kennels broke into cacophonous greeting, but there was no Stymie.

CHAPTER VI

As LEITHAN RETURNED to the house, still searching for Stymie, a voice from behind him startled him. "D'you know what's happened?"

He swung round and saw Sarah Pochard.

"I've been bitten." She held out her right hand so that he could see the drops of blood on her forefinger.

"I was trying to comb one of 'em and the bloody thing turned round and savaged me."

"Have you seen Stymie?" he demanded.

She allowed her anger to surface. "You don't care if it bleeding well took my head off, do you?"

"I rather gather it hasn't."

"You don't worry yourself what's happened. I'm quittin'. I hate the bloody smelly things. If they was mine I'd drown 'em all. So you can get someone else to look after 'em and I want three quid for the half week."

"We require a week's notice," he said, as he forced himself to consider this new problem. "You can't leave just like this."

She put her hands on her ample hips. "And who's bloody well going to stop me?"

He took his wallet from his coat pocket and counted out three pounds. If he was buying peace, he was prepared to pay the price.

She grabbed the money. "Who'll take me into the station?"

"I'll arrange for a taxi."

"Tell 'em I want it soon."

"Do you think you could possibly manage to feed the dogs before you leave?"

She shrugged her shoulders. "I guess so. But what if it bites me again?"

He muttered something she did not catch, which was as well, and walked past her and towards the kennels.

She stared after him. Proper crazy, she thought.

: :   : :

Pamela Breslow joined the fingers of her hands together and "cracked" the joints. She disliked the noise, but the action helped to ease away some of the tiredness that came from having typed since seven-thirty that morning.

She looked at the untidy mound of letters on her left. In an average week, four hundred people wrote to the magazine and ripped back the covers from their hidden lives as they asked for help. She was one of a team of four who gave advice and were paid at the rate of two shillings for letters of one page, or three shillings for two pages. Good advice was measured by the yard.

She stared at the large patch of damp in the curved wall immediately opposite her. The local builder had diagnosed the trouble as lack of a damp course and had said that either one must be put in or else the floor must be concreted. She had saved enough to have the job done, but was not spending that money in case Charles left Evadne. If he did, they would need every penny they could find. Sometimes, she proudly thought he would find the courage; sometimes, she was dully certain he wouldn't. If he didn't, would she force the break between them as she had promised? She shivered.

It was strange to think back to the cocktail party at which they'd met. It had been held in an old Victorian house, since pulled down by a speculative builder who had replaced quaint pomposity with commercial ugliness. She had not wanted to go because the people at the average cocktail party made her either angry or sad, or both.

She had been introduced to Leithan as "Someone else who scribbles for a living" and before he had smiled, apologetically, she had decided that of all the people in the room, this tall, nearing middle-aged, somewhat sardonic-looking man was the last person she would willingly have met. When, casually, he had pointed out his wife to her, she had been certain he had married the fat and obviously pushful woman for her money: it had been a shock to discover that it was he who had the money.

Of course, life had to hit her hard a second time. She was over the tragedy of the death of her husband and had settled into a peaceful routine that suited her and in which there was no room for emotional involvement, when she had to fall in love with a married man; moreover, a married man who was eager for a divorce but who was unable to petition for one and who did not dare allow himself to be named the guilty party.

She wished to God there had never been a fortune. She was no talent scout, but she was ready to bet that if Charles were forced into the main stream of life his writing would improve until it was very good. He had an intellectual and sardonic approach to life which pleased the critics, and his work had the readability which was so essential. But his literary life was the life of many years ago, and it lacked any sense of wonder, misery, hope, or fear.

She jerked her mind back to the present and read through the next letter. Jean, aged fourteen, wanted to know what she could do to get her steady back who had promised always to be faithful and had given her a ring from a Xmas cracker, but who was now going out with Liz. It was easy to sneer, but Pamela never had. She was only too aware of the terror of private misery, which could never be absurd.

Into the typewriter she inserted a sheet of paper headed with the name of the magazine, a carbon and the copy paper. "Dear Jean, first of all you must realise that if your boy friend wishes to go out with Liz there is nothing . . ." She stopped typing. Once or twice she had been traitor enough to herself to wonder what Charles wanted from their love.

She lit a cigarette and as she blew out the match, she heard a car come to a halt outside. Presumably one of her friends, none of whom ever really seemed able to understand that working hours were working hours, even when not passed in a town office. She stood up and looked out of the window and drew in her breath sharply. It was Charles.

She watched him climb out of the car. As always, he

was dressed in a suit that looked every penny of its
sixty-five guineas. She liked men to be smart. She felt
all warm inside because it was Charles, and then she
suffered a sense of shock as she studied his face. He
looked as though something terrible had happened.

She opened the door. He came in, kicked the door
shut behind him, and then kissed her with a passion that
held in it a hint of desperation. His hands caressed her
back and pressed her against him as if he were scared she
was about to run away.

"Charles—what on earth's the matter?"

He hesitated for a second, then said: "I'm hungry."

"I thought Mrs. Andrews was going to turn up and cook
lunch for you even if it is Sunday?"

"She did, and I ate too much."

She understood. "God, you men!" she whispered.
"There's only one thing you're ever interested in."

"What else is there?"

She drew his face down until she could kiss him hard
and long, then she broke free and led the way into the
sitting-room. "Find a seat and throw everything out of
the way, just so long as you don't upset the letters.
That lot have been answered, this lot have to be answered
by midday to-morrow."

He lifted a number of copies of *The Saturday Evening
Post* out of the arm-chair, which was suffering from a
prolapse of the springs, and sat down.

She studied his face again. "What's wrong, Charles?"

"Nothing, apart from the famine."

"Something's wrong, or you wouldn't have looked like
that."

"How was I looking?"

"As if . . . I don't know how to describe it."

He tried to smile. "As an eminent novelist, you
shouldn't have any difficulty in finding the necessary
words."

"You know damn' well I'm nothing but a hack writer who lives on other people's words." She saw that his face had lost some of the expression of strain. "Has . . . has Evadne been very trying?" For once, she deliberately trod on forbidden ground.

"You might say so. Have you drink and food in the house?"

"Yes."

"Will you promise to keep me well supplied with both?"

"Are you by any chance asking to stay the night?"

"Only if I'm satisfied that the cuisine's suitable."

"You," she said, "are the most self-satisfied bastard I've ever met. I've a mind to kick you into the cold, just to show you that even a fallen woman like me has some self-respect."

: :   : :

At seven o'clock, Pamela put down her knitting—for her, knitting was a self-imposed misery that Leithan described as masochistic—and looked across the room. "Charles, it's getting on."

"Only a couple of hours to bed."

"If you don't shut up, I'll paste some cotton-wool round your chin and turn you into a billy goat."

He drank more Cinzano.

"Your car's still outside the house, Charles."

He stared at the round curtained window on the road-side. "Unless it's been stolen, yes."

"Aren't . . . aren't you going to drive it round to the woods?"

"It can stay where it is."

She tried to contain the racing excitement within her. "This isn't your idea of a funny, is it, Charles?"

"I'm not joking."

"Then why? What's made you decide?"

"What's it matter?" he asked harshly. "Aren't you going to kiss me?"

"Kiss you, you old billy goat? I'll kiss you until you scream for help and can't work up an appetite for a fortnight. God, Charles, I feel as if someone has injected sunshine into all my veins. I feel completely and gloriously mad. I could lasso the moon, or dig up the sea: I could dance naked in a frenzy before Bacchus."

"Now who's wearing the beard?" he demanded.

: :   : :

The Cuenca Club held its annual general meeting at the Bambridge Rooms in Jermyn Street. Normally, apart from the committee, there were only two or three members present to hear the chairman deal with the almost non-existent agenda, the hon. treasurer present the balance sheet, the hon. P.R.O. catalogue the appearances of Cuencas in the press, the hon. secretary of the show committee report on shows, and the hon. secretary comment on the graph of membership. On the 20th November, there were so many people that the room was overcrowded.

The eighteen chairs around the oblong table were occupied, as were the five uncomfortable wooden ones beyond it. Fourteen other people were having to stand, although a search was being made for further chairs.

Georgina Yerby had dressed with care and her suit— worn, but smart—went well with her thin, angular, figure. Her face was set in hard angry lines, and there were dark circles under her eyes. She was trying hard to be pleasant to everyone, but frequently the bitterness within her came to the surface. She hated so many of those who were present. She and her friend had started the club and worked hard for it and the breed. They had gained grudging recognition of the breed in the dog papers. They had cajoled, begged, and almost forced,

people to support and work for the club. Her friend had
bred their bitch and it was the finest Cuenca in the
country. They had seen the breed grow until it was given
a pair of C.C.s a year and although the judges refused to
award C.C.s to any of the dogs, her bitch—willed to her
by her dead friend—had gained the first two C.C.s.

Then money, in the person of Evadne Leithan, had
stepped in.

She had bulldozed her way wherever she wanted to go,
and it had soon become clear that her only object was
to use her money to gain success for herself: she was not
interested in the general welfare of the club. She had
gone to Spain and visited all the important Cuenca
breeders and had finally made a fool of herself by paying
two hundred guineas for a tri-colour. But she had had the
last laugh, as money always did. Through an oversight,
the breed specifications had not listed tri-colour as an
eliminating fault. She had won two C.C.s and all the
odds were in favour of her winning the vital third one—
unless, of course, tri-colours were barred.

To her eternal credit, Georgina Yerby had not been
responsible for the initial move to bar tri-colours. As
chairman, it was her duty to guide, not lead, even if to do
so was to see her own interests threatened. Her neutrality
had lasted until she discovered that Evadne Leithan had
gone so far as to try to buy votes, then she had fought back
with all of her—limited—resources. Her battle met with
some success. Although she had a cold nature and found
it difficult to make friends, no one doubted her honest
sincerity and that fact brought her supporters. But how
well could sincerity match money? This meeting would
tell and she was terrified that she knew the answer.

Leithan arrived and went down the stairs to the room
in which the meeting was being held.

"There you are."

He turned to face Alan Marsh.

"Where's Evadne?"

"Isn't she here?"

"She hasn't been near our place and Judy went to no end of trouble getting special food in, knowing Evadne likes her eats." Marsh fingered his lips. "Has she said why she didn't come to us?"

Marsh was looking very worried, thought Leithan. Wondering if he were no longer *persona grata* and if the friendship that meant so much to his toadying soul had come to an end? "I thought she must be with you since I haven't seen her since she went to London."

Judy Marsh hurried up to her husband's side. She was a bird-like woman who used too much lipstick.

"He hasn't seen her," said her husband. He finally let go of his lips.

"You haven't seen Evadne?" asked Judy Marsh.

Leithan shook his head.

"Where is she?" said Marsh. "She's got to be here, I tell you, she's got to be here."

"She will be," replied Leithan.

"I hope nothing's happened to her," said Judy Marsh.

"Something must have done." Marsh's voice was both angry and uncertain. "Look at all the special eats we bought."

"We're not worried about that," snapped his wife, and she looked angrily at him. "We're concerned about dear Evadne. I couldn't bear it if anything happened to her. We're so fond of her."

Leithan offered them cigarettes. As he shut his gold cigarette-case, he saw Marsh staring at it and mentally assessing its worth. For Marsh, everything could be reduced to pounds, shillings, and pence. Leithan said he wanted to have a word with someone and he managed to break free from them.

Georgina Yerby, at the far end of the table, stood up and called for silence. Then, she welcomed everyone to the fifth annual general meeting. As she spoke, in a high-pitched and wearying voice, her gaze constantly went to the door at the far end of the room.

The balance sheet for the year was passed and the committee were returned unopposed.

Mrs. Cyclen presented her P.R. report. "In the past year, we have gained mentions in the national press on no less than three occasions which I feel certain is a remarkable achievement." She looked for, and received, some applause. "The first two references concerned the shows at Crufts and Glasgow when Cuencas appeared in the list of winners, while the third one followed an accident in Kensington High Street between a taxi and a bus. I know you'll all be glad to hear that although the Cuenca suffered severe shock from the noise the bus made when it crashed into the taxi and the taxi turned over, she is now very much better. The press referred to a Pekinese as being the cause of the bus swerving, and although I immediately got on to the papers and told them the dog was a Cuenca, they very rudely refused to print the correction. However . . ."

Marsh tiptoed up to where Leithan was standing. "She's still not here."

"I know," replied Leithan.

"But when Mrs. Cyclen's finished, we'll start on the agenda and the first item is tri-colours."

"She'll get here in time."

"But what say if she don't? I've been speaking to one or two of those we've persuaded down. They're saying that if she can't be bothered to turn up, they can't be bothered to vote. I'm telling you, they're proper fed up. Where is she? You must know."

"I don't."

"I'll go and see if she's somewhere upstairs." Marsh turned and hurried out of the room.

Georgina Yerby watched Marsh leave.

". . . And I have persuaded a very well-known firm of doggie food manufacturers," continued Mrs. Cyclen, "to feature a Cuenca in their advertisements when our first champion is made up." She paused for a few seconds. "I do hope you think our small sub-committee has done its job?" She stared anxiously round herself, as if expecting a demand for her immediate resignation.

Mrs. Cyclen was assured by everybody's appreciation. Georgina Yerby announced they would now deal with the proposals listed on the agenda. Immediately, the atmosphere became tense, strained, and angry.

"The first item reads—'That the breed standards be altered so as to exclude tri-colours and that the Kennel Club be so notified.' " Georgina Yerby looked at the doorway.

Marsh ran into the room and crossed to Leithan's side. "She's nowhere. She's not turning up. What am I going to say to people?"

Leithan made no answer.

The opposers to the motion had been relying on Evadne Leithan to be the spearhead of the attack: they were prepared to follow. With no one to lead them, they were uncertain and largely disorganised.

The vote was taken. Fifteen members were in favour of the motion, eight were against, and there were twelve abstentions. It was victory for the old guard.

CHAPTER VII

LEITHAN WAS CUTTING up raw paunch and the smell of it disgusted him as it always did. From the tack room, he could look through the line of wire-mesh doors and see the drooling dogs as they regarded him with desperate appeal. He suffered a desire to take them out and shoot them.

"Anyone around?" called out a voice from outside.

"In here." Leithan put down the large butcher's knife on the wooden slab. A young man, in his middle twenties, entered the building.

"Are you Mr. Leithan?"

The dogs began to yowl as they forgot their stomachs long enough to realise a stranger was present.

Leithan shouted at the dogs and they reluctantly became silent. "I am."

"My name's Detective-Constable Herald. I'd like to check on something with you, sir?"

Leithan picked up the knife. "I'll finish this first."

"Of course, sir." Herald stared at the paunch. "What is it?"

"This?" Leithan cut through a roll of the green, blubbery mass. "Have you never sampled the delights of tripe and onions?"

"Not half. My mum used to be a dab hand at that."

"This is the raw material."

The detective looked at Leithan's face to see if he were joking, then back at the paunch. "That is?"

"Yes."

Herald remained suspicious.

Leithan finished cutting up the paunch into small squares and apportioned it into the plastic bowls. "I'll just feed these ravenous beasts." He picked up the six bowls, one on top of the other, and opened each wire door in turn and put the food in the compartment. As soon as he returned, he washed the rubber gloves under the tap and then peeled them off.

"What are they?" asked Herald, indicating with a vague wave of his beefy right arm the dogs, who could be heard guzzling their food and repeatedly choking.

"Cuencas. A Spanish breed of dog, reputed to have

been the favourite of the Infanta of Philip the Fourth. If so, the Spanish have got their own back on us for the Armada." He led the way out of the kennels.

They went behind the ornamental trees—two of the evergreens were bright with small orange berries—and round the garage to the door of the house. Herald showed no interest in the building. If anything, Leithan guessed, the other was scornful of such age. Once in the sitting-room, Leithan said: "What's the trouble?"

"We've had a report, sir, that Mrs. Leithan is missing. We're wondering if there's any truth in it?"

"No, there isn't."

"Then she's here now, sir?"

"No. She's been a little under the weather recently and I imagine she just hasn't bothered to write me."

"D'you know where she is?"

"Not at this precise moment."

"You think she's on holiday and hasn't got round yet to writing you?"

"Yes."

"When did you last see her, sir?"

"When I drove her into Ashford on Sunday to catch a train. I dropped her at the station."

"To go on this holiday?"

"Not quite. She was due to stay with some acquaintances of hers who live in London."

"Would they be Mr. and Mrs. Marsh?"

"How have you got their names?"

"They made the report, sir. Proper worried, he said he was."

"I can imagine."

"It sounds as if you don't like them, sir?"

"I doubt whether my likes or dislikes matter at the moment."

Herald's expression tightened. "They say she wasn't at a meeting she was absolutely certain to attend."

E

"The certainty was demonstrably false, wasn't it?"

"You're not at all worried?"

"My wife is an adult of sound mind. Does that answer you?"

"No, sir."

"I presume that in the present instance she needed a break and therefore took it. Likewise, when she decides she's had enough, she'll come back."

"Is she in good health?"

"She suffers from *angina pectoris*. However, provided she takes everything easily and overdoes nothing, she's all right."

"Have you checked with hospitals, sir?"

"No."

"Wouldn't that be an idea?"

"It would if there was any reason to suppose she might be in one. As there isn't, I haven't bothered."

"I see, sir." Herald stood up. "Let us know when you hear from her, will you?" He crossed to the door. "Thanks for your help, Mr. Leithan."

Leithan stood in the middle of the room. He heard the front door open and then shut. Slowly, he lit a cigarette.

: :   : :

The detective-inspector's room was on the first floor of the police station and it reflected a little of the D.I.'s character. It was always faintly untidy, but in a manner that did not affect efficiency, and on the far wall was a calendar featuring a young lady whose vital statistics were open to inspection. The D.I. was a cheerful person whose record was neither brilliant nor black—he claimed that had it been either there would have been no chance of further promotion for him—and he managed to retain his sense of humour despite a morose detective-superintendent called Murch who suffered from a duodenal ulcer. The D.I. was almost bald, a physical feature that made him appear far older than his thirty-eight years.

Herald knocked on the door of his office and when there was no answer he went in. He crossed to the desk and looked down at the papers and read through the top ones to see if they contained anything of interest. He heard approaching footsteps and stepped back from the desk. Jaeger entered.

"I thought you must have gone home," said the D.I., as he sat down and took a battered pipe from his pocket.

"It's three miles out to the place, sir."

"And I suppose you walked 'em?" The D.I. opened up a plastic pouch and began to press tobacco into the bowl of his pipe. "What's the verdict? Much ado about nothing? The shower in London never have been able to sort the wheat from the chaff."

Herald twisted one of the two wooden chairs round so that he could sit down. "I don't know."

"That's honest, even if it doesn't make for a good start."

"He's rolling, lives in one of those old dumps that's all cobwebs and history. And he's most superior and sky-high on his dignity."

"What's the matter? Didn't he offer you a drink?" The D.I. struck a match and sucked flame into his pipe. His juniors said that he was busy trying to ape Maigret, but they made certain they said it behind his back because beneath his genial exterior there was a hard core of something that was very close to ruthlessness.

"He spoke about his wife as if she was almost a stranger. Know what I mean, sir?"

"Perhaps."

Herald ran his fingers through his crinkly hair. "He was on edge, but for a bloke whose wife's missing and has *angina*, he wasn't nearly worried enough."

"Maybe he objected to you?"

Herald took a boiled sweet from his coat pocket and unwrapped it. "I asked him if he'd been on to any hospitals."

"And?"

"Said he hadn't. That one stinks, doesn't it?"

The D.I.'s pipe went out and he had to strike three matches before he relit it. "When did he last see her?"

"He drove her into the station on Sunday to catch the London train. Presumably, the one she wasn't on when it arrived."

"Did he see her into the train?"

"All he said was, he dropped her at the station. When he heard she hadn't arrived, he just reckoned she'd changed her mind about stopping with those people and had decided to go on holiday."

"Where to?"

Herald shrugged his shoulders.

The D.I. picked up one of the crime reports on his desk and read it through. He looked up. "Hasn't Leery, in all his twenty years in the force, yet learned that burglary consists of breaking *and* entering?" He tapped the paper with the stem of his pipe. "Give this back to Leery and tell him to do the job properly." He flicked the sheet of paper over the desk and with an acrobatic lunge, Herald managed to catch it. "What are you doing at the moment?"

"I was on the stolen car, sir."

"Which one? They're always being stolen."

"Aldington. The detention centre lot."

"Those young bastards. Tell Leery to take over. You have a look into this business of Mrs. Leithan. It's a thousand pounds to a penny they've had a row and she's gone home to Mother, but just in case, sniff around. See how the land lies between them and whether he's got any little bit of fluff tucked away out of sight. If it looks promising, have a word with the banks and persuade them to tell you whether she's been drawing money since the eighteenth or whether she's taken out a large sum prior to that date. See about hospitals and what the railway people have to say. You know the form."

"Right, sir." Herald stood up. He put the boiled sweet in his mouth.

"And don't forget to be more discreet than you were the last time you went blundering after a missing person."

Herald silently swore as he turned angrily away. Wasn't he ever to be allowed to forget that he had once failed to be quite as diplomatic as he ought to have been?

: :   : :

Ashford railway station was being repaired and a pneumatic drill was spasmodically hammering away as Herald made his way over the bridge to the up platform. He approached the barrier and the drill started once more. The ticket collector motioned with his clippers. Herald shook his head. "Police," he shouted.

The drill ceased.

"Police," repeated Herald.

The drill resumed.

A woman impatiently pushed past Herald and held out her ticket to be clipped. The drill ceased.

Herald managed to speak several consecutive words to the ticket collector, who called in a companion to whom he handed over his job; then he and Herald went along the platform to a temporary wooden hut that was three-quarters of the way along the platform. Inside, a paraffin stove was burning unevenly and filling the place with acrid fumes. The ticket collector warmed his hands by the stove. "It's ruddy cold to-day, in spite of the sun."

Herald did not bother to appear to commiserate with

the other, he was careless of woes that did not directly concern him. "Who was clipping tickets for the eleven forty-two on the eighteenth?"

"Jeeze, mate, I ain't the memory man."

"It was last Sunday, when we had all the fog." Herald studied his reflection in the battered mirror that hung on the wall and patted down the front of his hair.

"Then! I was. And a bleeding day that was, with nothing on time and everyone running round in circles."

"D'you remember a woman with a mucky kind of a dog? First class, wouldn't mind betting."

"What d'you mean by mucky?"

"It's small and called a Cuenca. Looks as if you'd belted it up the backside and its face had smashed into a concrete wall."

"One of them that was on the telly the other day and bit Stanley Dangerfield?"

"How the hell should I know? D'you think I've time to watch?"

The railwayman slowly shook his head. "That wasn't what you've just said: it was a skipper something or other."

"Then let's forget it."

"You ain't talking about the Leithan bitch, are you? That fat old cow?"

"How the hell?" demanded Herald.

"Two months ago, almost to the day, I was collecting tickets and a fat woman comes panting up to me and tears me off a regular strip for making her climb up and down all them steps over the bridge. Being a peaceful sort of bloke, I just said them steps were put up without my permission, but she snorts and begins to ask me for me name and says she was going to get me hung, drawn, and quartered. I moves me foot and quite by accident, like, I kicks the thing she's got on a lead. There's a noise like a stuck pig and my leg gets bitten. I was about to let fly and give her what for, when she lams into me for kicking her darling dog and before I knows what's what she's called the station-master and is yelling for me to be sent to jug for cruelty. 'Course, no one took no notice of her."

Herald allowed himself the luxury of another boiled sweet. "How about last Sunday? D'you see her catch the eleven forty-two?"

"Not her. I ain't seen her for a month or more. Dropped down dead, has she? If so, I'll buy me old woman a drink to-night."

Herald quite spoiled the other's pleasure by explaining that, in so far as anyone knew, Mrs. Leithan had not dropped down dead.

: :   : :

Leithan walked round the edge of the easterly woods and as he came to the gateway in the hedge there was a clatter of wings, the harsh staccato cry of alarm, and a cock pheasant rocketed away from the hedge, voiding as it went. He watched it swing right and disappear behind the nearer wood, a glorious living mosaic of browns, greens, blacks, whites, and violets.

He was close to the boundary of his land and beyond was the twenty-acre kale field of his neighbour. He had always wanted to buy the next-door farm and had long since promised it to himself should it come on the market.

He began to walk in a broad sweep that would bring him to the cow-sheds. Deakin knew how to make use of every square foot of land without destroying any of it. No hedges had been ripped up, no trees had been felled simply because they upset the growth of grass beneath them. Deakin, in a subconscious manner, thought as Leithan did. The countryside was a valued heritage to be passed on as nearly as possible in the form in which it had been received.

Leithan went down to the small stream, surprisingly

short of water, and climbed the opposite slope on which bracken still grew, despite the fact it was cut at least twice a year. He reached the top of the slope and stopped, to look along his land, then went on to the cow-sheds where he watched Deakin and Alf Petrie as they milked the Jerseys.

He returned to the house, amidst a yowling chorus from the dogs, and told Mrs. Andrews he would not be in for tea. She understood Evadne to be on holiday and was looking after him with possessive efficiency.

He drove to the village of Cleariton and stopped at the general store which still seemed to make a living for its owner despite the rash of supermarkets in the towns. He bought a pound box of chocolates.

He arrived at Pamela's house and gave her the chocolates.

"And what about my figure?" she asked, as she closed the door behind him.

"I'll grant it a detailed testimonial any time you want."

"You know perfectly well, Mr. Charles Leithan, that I asked you not to buy me any more chocolates because my spare tyre already looks half-inflated."

"Then use some will-power and hand them back." He grinned as he held out his hand.

"Like hell," she replied.

They went through to the sitting-room and for once it was tidy. Obviously, the mess had at last become too much for her and she had cleared it up. Now, the room would slowly be allowed to become untidy once more. He kissed her.

"What's that in aid of?" she asked. Her brown eyes expressed malicious enjoyment.

"A formal greeting."

"I keep my two cheeks for that."

He put his arm round her waist and, unaware of

THE BENEFITS OF DEATH

what he was doing, held her so tightly against him that
she was almost off balance. She looked up at his face
and saw that the expression she could not read was back
on his face.

"We're off to Brighton," he said.

"Brighton?"

"I thought we'd treat ourselves to a night out."

"You don't have to take me out, Charles. I'm quite
happy here with you."

He shook his head impatiently and released her waist.
"A touch of the bright lights would do us both a power of
good."

"D'you honestly think you'll find them in Brighton in
November?"

"We can try. In any case, since we're not married,
they'll put out the welcome mats." He walked across to
the small table on which were some bottles and a soda
siphon. "What's yours?"

"Gin and tonic, please." She reflected that for the
first time in the two years she had known him, he was
acting as though he needed to drink. The previous night,
he had become almost incoherent before they finally
went to bed.

He handed her a glass. "Here's cheers." He drank
deeply.

"Any word from Evadne?" she asked.

He finished his drink. "No."

"It's getting rather odd, isn't it?"

"Why?"

She shrugged her shoulders. "I should have thought
you'd have heard something by now. A pompous note
from solicitors telling you your wife was divorcing you."

"Not a thing."

"Has she still got Stymie?"

"Yes."

"Bully for Stymie."

"What's that supposed to mean?"

"Nothing, Charles. Why are you so jumpy?"

He forced himself to speak more calmly. "The coming of spring."

"Spring's a hell of a long way off, even if your thoughts are always turned towards it."

He poured himself out another drink. She tried not to worry, but failed.

Ten minutes later, they left the house and drove towards the Tenterden Road. "We'll go through Hawkhurst. I can't stand the coast road with all the faceless hotels of Hastings and Bexhill looking out on to a dirty sea."

"And yet we're heading for Brighton?"

"It's a town of vice. The hotels have painted faces, the harlot's trade-mark."

"And that's attractive?"

"Of course."

"You're being an absolute swine," she said bitterly. She waited for an apology that she was certain would not come.

Leithan slowed down behind a bus and was almost blinded by the undipped lights of an oncoming car.

"Charles . . ." she began, and then became silent.

The car passed them and he overtook the bus. He looked very quickly at her, and the reflected light from the instrument panel was just sufficient to show him her face. She looked very open to hurt. He rested his left hand on her knees. "I love you."

"I know and it makes me sing inside every hour of every day." She paused, then spoke quickly. "You are certain you want her to learn, aren't you?"

"Learn what?"

"That you and I are shacking up together."

"You get hold of some awful expressions!"

"That one's long out of date. But you are certain, aren't you?"

"Of course. Why d'you have to ask?"

"Because . . . because I think the house is being watched."

The car suddenly swerved and she cried out.

"Sorry. Something on the road."

There had been nothing on the road.

"I saw a Mini car parked back from the house yesterday afternoon. I noticed it because its registration letters were PAM. I saw it again to-day."

"Cars are everywhere these days."

"There isn't a house nearer than mine to where it was. I asked Old Moore if he knew anything about it and he thought it belonged to a man who'd been inquiring in the village where I lived. Yet no one's called on me."

He wished he had not suggested Brighton. The journey suddenly seemed futile and ridiculous.

CHAPTER VIII

HERALD ARRIVED at the police station at eight o'clock and said good morning to Detective-Constable Leery. He held the other man in contempt because Leery was middle-aged and so clearly a failure. Herald respected only the successful.

He went into the general room that he, Leery and the P.C. seconded to C.I.D. duties used, and looked at his desk to see if any messages had been left. There was none. He took a sweet from his pocket, unwrapped it, and sucked it. The buzzer from the D.I. sounded and he hurried through to the other's office.

"Well," said Jaeger, "how's the Leithan case?"

Herald used his tongue to place the sweet between his top gum and his cheek. "Waiting for the banks to start up, sir, and then I'll phone round and see where she keeps her lolly."

The D.I. picked up a pencil and fiddled with it. "From what you've told me, this chap Leithan's taking his wife's disappearance with unnatural calm?"

"Quite."

"If she'd dropped down dead, there'd be a body: in the train, in the street, in a hotel. There'd also be a dog loose. If she really is on holiday, why hasn't she let him know by now? And what's she wearing?"

"She had a few things with her, sir, since she was going to stay with those people in London."

The D.I. dropped the pencil. "He says he left her at the station to catch the train, but we can be pretty certain she didn't go on to the platform. Why not? Why should she suddenly change her mind? And why didn't he see her on to the train?"

"No manners."

"If you'd any sense you'd know he's the kind of man always to do the right thing. Herald, I'll have a word with the banks. You get on to the local policeman and find out if he knows of any girl friends.

"I spoke to the super about the case last night and he said the Leithans had lived in the area for some time; the father used to live at Great Chart and made a fortune at something or other. That suggests it's him who's got the money, not her. Tell you what: after you've done the other chore, ring round the Ashford solicitors and find out which, if any, manages the family affairs. If you get tied up, tell Watters to handle that one."

"Right, sir."

"And get it clear from the start that you're only asking and not demanding. None of your bulls-in-a-china-shop."

"Mustn't annoy his lordship too much?" sneered Herald.

"Not unless you want to become a civilian and find out how difficult it is to earn an honest living," replied the D.I., with pleasant good humour, underneath which was the snap of command.

: :   : :

The bank manager greeted Jaeger with a wariness that came from the experience of previous police inquiries. Jaeger spoke as he sat down. "One of my chaps was on to you earlier, asking whether you handled Mrs. Leithan's account and you said you did."

The manager nodded.

"I haven't come for any secrets, you'll be glad to hear." Jaeger grinned. He had a warm personality that made him likable and liked.

"I'll believe you. Later." The manager pushed across a silver cigarette-box. "D'you smoke?"

"A pipe. But I won't light up in here in case your customers complain."

"They very rarely do," said the other, in an unusual attempt at humour.

"I'm wondering whether Mrs. Leithan drew a largish sum of money just before the eighteenth, or whether she's drawn any since then?"

"Is something wrong?"

"Quite frankly, we don't know yet."

"Wouldn't Mr. Leithan be the one to help you?"

"Not just at the moment."

The manager sighed. "All right. I won't give you any figures, of course, but I'll do what I can." He lifted one of the three telephone receivers on his desk and spoke to someone. When he replaced the receiver, he helped himself to a cigarette. "They're a very nice family. Been with this bank for three generations now."

There was a knock on the door and a man came in. He handed a piece of paper to the manager, then left. The manager read what was written on the paper, looked up. "Mrs. Leithan has drawn on neither of her two accounts in the past seven days."

"What was the last withdrawal for?"

"A reasonably small sum and in accordance with her usual practice."

"Will you give me a buzz if there's any movement in her account? And d'you know if she banks anywhere else or if she has a Post Office Savings account?"

"So far as I know, we're her only bankers."

: :   : :

As Jaeger returned to his room at the station, Herald hurried in. Jaeger noted how eager the other was to show his keen efficiency.

"I was on to the Cleariton sub-station just now, sir."

The D.I. sat down behind his desk and produced his pipe.

"It was the last of eight, including the one at Piltonhurst."

"Shall I make a note of that for the promotions board?"

Herald was proof against sarcasm. "The constable says a man whose description fits Leithan like a glove is a frequent visitor at a place belonging to a Mrs. Breslow. She's a widow. He thinks the late husband was in oil."

"I doubt whether that aspect of the matter will concern us." Jaeger lit his pipe. "What's she like?"

"Very bedable."

The pipe was going well for once and the D.I. was surrounded by clouds of smoke. "Has Leithan been there recently?"

"A Sunbeam Rapier was parked outside the house all night on the eighteenth."

"When the cat's away . . . Go and see the constable and get all you can out of him and then report back to me." Jaeger began to see the pattern of the case and, as always happened, he felt excited. He wondered what kind of people these were, people who at the present were only names to him. The man might be short, tall, thin, fat, ugly, handsome. The wife was a bitch. The widow was "bedable." It was a game of chess that might not be a game. People vanished every day of the week and many of them were never heard of again, but investigations made it perfectly clear they had disappeared voluntarily. Mrs. Leithan might be one of those. Or she might have gone on an unannounced holiday, as her husband insisted. Or she might have been taken suddenly ill and had not, as yet, been identified. Or it might be a game of chess in which the pieces would slowly change into people.

: :   : :

Leithan was trying to work when he heard the ring of the front-door bell. He swore. For days, the words had refused to come and he was so conscious of this failure that they retreated even further. Not for the first time, he wondered why he gave in to the compulsion to write. It only brought him pain. He laughed with others when his books were discussed, but secretly he nearly cried. Part of him went into each book and when it failed it was part of him that failed.

He heard the mumble of voices and the clacking of Mrs. Andrews's shoes on the brick floor of the hall. She knocked on the door of the study and looked inside, an expression close to fear on her face. She regarded his ability to write as miraculous, and had a superstitious dread of interrupting a miracle. "I'm terribly sorry to bother you, Mr. Leithan, but there's a man says he wants to see you. He's a detective."

Leithan pushed his typewriter away from himself.

"What's he want?" As soon as he had spoken, he knew the words were useless.

"I . . . I don't know," she replied, flustered.

He stood up. "All right."

"I told him you was working, Mr. Leithan, and how you was never disturbed . . ."

He managed to still her fear at what she had done and then he went into the hall. He saw a man, studying the collection of arms, who at first seemed well into middle-age because of his nearly bald head, but who was obviously much less aged when he smiled.

"Mr. Leithan? I'm Detective-Inspector Jaeger. Sorry to bother you like this." He gestured at the pistols. "What a wonderful collection you've got."

"Not too bad."

"I used to want to do the same, but when the prices climbed to the skies I had to make do with seeing them in the museums. That one up there . . . That's a very early Colt, isn't it?"

Leithan's voice quickened, as it always did when discussing guns. "A Dragoon. It's one of the first models, forty-four calibre. I spotted that in a shop in Lewes. The chap wanted twenty-five pounds for it and after a stern struggle I beat him down to twenty."

"Twenty?"

Leithan smiled briefly. "You picked out my best buy. Just to keep the records straight, there's that pepperbox up there which I congratulated myself on until I discovered four other pistols had been cannibalised to make it."

"If it was my collection, I'd be afraid to leave it hanging there."

"What's one to do? Hide it away or see it, insure it, and risk? I'd do the same if I had a dozen Gauguins."

Jaeger reluctantly looked away from the pistols.

"You'll have guessed, sir, that I've come along to see if you've heard anything from Mrs. Leithan?"

"I've heard nothing."

"I suppose you're beginning to get a little worried?"

"I'm certain she's still on holiday."

"Even though you took her in to Ashford to catch a train for London to attend a meeting that meant so much to her, but which she didn't go to?"

"If she's on holiday, she obviously wouldn't have gone to it."

"Mrs. Marsh declared that she'd never have missed it willingly?"

"We don't all act as other people think we should."

"That's true enough."

"I'm grateful for the agreement."

"By the way, did you see your wife on to the train?"

"Didn't that other policeman tell you that I left her by the booking office?"

The D.I. continued to speak with unabated good humour. "I suppose you've checked with a number of hospitals by now?"

"No. It isn't necessary."

"Maybe not, sir. Still, I take it you won't mind if we have a quick check?"

"Are you giving me the option, or presenting me with an ultimatum?"

Jaeger laughed. "Words can mean anything, can't they?" He looked around the hall. "Wonderful old place you've got here."

Leithan answered automatically and talked about the house and the ash-staked mad room in the loft—a moderately common feature of Kent houses—in which legend said a woman had been incarcerated for fifteen years and whose screams could be heard even as far away as the Piltonhurst rectory.

F

The telephone rang. Leithan excused himself and answered it.

"Charles—the police have just been here."

He stared out at the garden. For a moment, all was motionless. Old Bill Wren—as stubborn as hell—remained bending over the middle of the left-hand herbaceous border: the dead leaves in the beech hedges ceased to rustle to the wind that was sweeping in from the south: the tall oak tree in the centre of the east wood became frozen: the heavy pot-bellied clouds hung lifeless in the sky: the robin became a statue on the edge of the bird bath. Then, all was movement again. "Why?" he said.

"There were two of them. Our local bobby and a young chap in a revoltingly-coloured sports jacket."

"Damn the clothes. What did they want?"

"To find out whether I knew you and if so, for how long. From the way the young man leered at me, he also would have liked to ask me whether I'd go to bed with him."

"God Almighty," shouted Leithan. "I'll have him sacked. Did he say anything?"

"He didn't quite have the nerve." Her voice faltered slightly. "But he was mentally undressing me all the time."

"Have they gone?"

"Just before I phoned."

"I'll be right over."

"There's nothing to do now, Charles, but I had to tell you."

"I'm coming over."

"Charles . . . where is Evadne?"

He slammed the receiver down, swung round and spoke wildly to Jaeger. "Your bloody men have been worrying Mrs. Breslow and one of 'em's been insulting her. I'll write to the chief constable."

"What precisely did he say, sir?"

"He didn't say anything, but spent the whole time mentally undressing her."

Jaeger relaxed slightly.

"What right have you to worry her? Who said you could? Why are you worrying her?"

"I'd have thought the reason was obvious, sir."

"Not to me, it isn't."

"I expect it soon will be," said the detective quietly.

CHAPTER IX

HERALD SAT DOWN and stared at the electric convector heater. The day was cold and damp and the heater did little to relieve either feature. He sucked a boiled sweet and thought about a pal of his who was knocking back thirty quid a week up in a Midlands car factory. And whipping various bits and pieces off the assembly line with which he optimistically hoped eventually to be able to build his own car. Herald wanted a car more than anything else in the world. The modern birds were getting so status-conscious they wouldn't begin to look at a man without a reasonable car.

The buzzer summoned him to the D.I.'s room.

"Well?" said Jaeger.

"Not at all bad looking, sir, and must give the old boy a wonderful roll in bed. Wouldn't mind taking her on myself, come to that."

"So she gathered." Jaeger's voice was hard. "You'll keep your sex life to yourself and not parade it around in working hours or I'll slam a disciplinary charge on you. Is that clear?"

Herald became sullen.

"What did she have to say?" asked Jaeger.

"That they were just good friends."

"And?"

"And nothing, sir. All else she did was to get rather desperate as she tried to convince me."

Jaeger made no comment.

"Something else happened, sir." Herald had forgotten his resentment and was now eager to prove his own worth. "I used a bucket-load of initiative."

Jaeger looked suspicious.

"When I was driving the local P.C. back to his place I saw a tall man in a tiny car. Remember Mr. Abraham Smith?"

The D.I. stared out of the window at the unsightly jumble of buildings beyond. "The private detective?"

"Retired detective-sergeant from the Devon police. He's been watching Pamela Breslow."

"Divorce?"

"That's it in one, sir. He's been on and off the job since the beginning of September, trying to land our bloke in a compromising position—I wonder if they ever actually do?"

"Could you elevate your mind just for a short while?"

"He says Leithan's been a frequent visitor, but that before the eighteenth he always left early on in the evening. On the eighteenth, Leithan's car was parked slap outside the front door all night. And that's happened since then."

"Who's Smith working for?"

"Podermare and Co., in Tenterden. They told him their client didn't mind how much it cost her, she wanted proof her husband was committing adultery. She even gave the dates on which the Breslow house was to be watched."

"See 'em and check." The D.I. produced his pipe and

tobacco pouch and then found the latter was empty. His normally cheerful expression became sour. "And in the meantime, get me an ounce of Player's tawny navy cut. Tawny, don't forget." He was silent for a few seconds. "We're missing the key at the moment. I wonder where the hell it is?"

: :   : :

Leithan arrived at Pamela's house as heavy rain began to fall from the leaden skies. He ran from the car to the slight shelter of the small open porch and waited for her to open the door.

As soon as he was in the house, he said: "What did the bastards want?"

She put her hands round the back of his neck and kissed him. "Please, Charles, please keep calm. You must."

"When some bloody little whipper-snapper comes along and ogles you?"

"What does that matter?" She swallowed heavily. "Charles, he's almost certain you and I are lovers."

"So what if he is?" Leithan freed himself from her and began to pace the square hall. "It's none of their business. What did he say? I told the inspector I'd report him."

"What inspector?"

"Came out from Ashford and asked me a lot of impertinent questions. What did this man say to you?"

She shook her head in a gesture of despair. What did it matter? The detective wasn't the first man to have sized her up in terms of bed-potential. "Charles, what were they at your place for? What impertinent questions were they asking?"

"Whether I'd checked with the hospitals."

"What did you tell them?"

"That I hadn't, of course."

She moistened her lips. "Why . . . why haven't you been checking, Charles?"

He swung round. "Why should I? Evadne's on holiday, not ill. I know what they're thinking—you don't have to spell it out for me. Just because she didn't turn up at the bloody Cuenca meeting. . . ." He stopped. "Do you believe I've killed her?"

She shivered. "Stop it and calm down. I know you couldn't do such a thing, no matter how much you wanted to."

"Who said I wanted to?"

"I didn't mean it that way."

"Or did your tongue say what you'd been thinking?"

"Please, Charles, please don't attack me. I only know one thing and that's that I love you, and when you're like this it hurts me deeply."

He spoke very slowly and very softly, so that his voice was little more than a whisper. "You don't hate me, Pam, do you?"

She began to cry.

: :   : :

Detective-Sergeant Watters always seemed to be wearing clothes that had fitted him before he grew the last half-inch, and as he made his way into the solicitor's office his coat looked as if the seams at the shoulders might part at any moment. He was asked to wait and it was fifteen minutes before the receptionist took him up to Enty's office. As he shook hands with the solicitor, he wondered how much the other's multi-coloured waistcoat had cost and whether it needed much courage to wear it. "Glad to find you working on a Saturday morning, sir."

"You may be, I'm not," replied Enty. "What the devil's going to happen to my golf handicap?"

Watters grinned.

"For several years now, Sergeant, I've been trying to persuade the solicitors of Kent that if they all closed their doors on Saturdays, the public would be forced to come to them during the week. But being an honourable profession, Brutus, they're all scared that if there were such a pact one of their number would renege, open his doors wide, and so steal not only a march, but also many highly valued clients. Hence, we all work on Saturdays."

"It's rather nice to meet a fellow sufferer."

"Your sympathy alarms me. Remind me to cross-examine you unmercifully the next time we clash in court."

"You didn't do too badly last time, sir. You called me a liar at least five times."

"Was that all? For some unaccountable reason, I must have been feeling kindly towards you." Enty leaned back in his chair. "Well. What's the trouble?"

"Do you handle Mr. Leithan's affairs, sir?"

"Yes."

"We'd like a run down on them."

"Quite possibly."

"What about his will and his wife's?"

"What about them?"

"What are the terms?"

"My dear Sergeant, until you can force me to speak, my clients' business is their affair and not yours. So return to your detective-inspector and tell him that."

"Come on, sir, you know as well as I do that we can go to Somerset House and look up the father's will."

"Quite so, but until misfortune overtakes them, not Mr. and Mrs. Leithan's will."

Watters sighed very obviously. "All right, I'll just take the father's. I said to the old man we wouldn't get anything more out of you—shouldn't have pulled you in for speeding last year."

"That would cost you dearly for slander if only there were witnesses." Enty's expression changed slightly. "What are all the inquiries in aid of?"

"We don't know quite yet, sir. That's one of the things we're trying to find out."

"You'll get the terms of the will from me and nothing more. D'you want the exact wording, or will you accept a résumé?"

"Yours will do, sir, if it's accurate."

"The capital was left on trust. The interest to Charles Leithan until married and then jointly to him and his wife. On the death of either party, the capital vests absolutely in the survivor and any children. If there is a divorce, the capital vests absolutely in the innocent party."

"How much is the capital?"

"At the death of Reginald Leithan, the father, it stood at about a hundred and twenty thousand pounds—after death duties were paid."

"How's the money invested?"

"In a number of ways."

"Unless it's all in Government securities, it must have appreciated a lot?"

"Perhaps."

It was obvious that the interview was at an end. Watters thanked Enty with elaborate care, as if he had been granted complete co-operation, and Enty replied with mild sarcasm. Watters left. Because he had not dealt with the Leithan case before, he had no idea what Jaeger would make of the meagre information. He wondered what sort of a queer coot the old man Leithan must have been to have inserted the divorce clause in the trust.

: :   : :

Detective-Superintendent Murch was commonly referred to as The Scourge. His subordinates took almost as much interest in his duodenal ulcer as he did, since it so largely governed his relationship with them.

Between Jaeger and Murch there generally existed a truce, drawn up—although never acknowledged—because otherwise there would have been continuous friction between two people of such differing characteristics. Where Jaeger saw light, Murch saw dark, where Jaeger saw promise, Murch saw misery.

Murch sat in the divisional superintendent's room on the ground floor, and sucked a tablet. The uniformed superintendent and the D.I. watched him. "All right, so she appears to be missing. You've been on to hospitals, nursing homes, mortuaries, the lot. She didn't attend a meeting everyone swears she'd have left her death-bed to attend. She hasn't drawn a penny from the bank since she went missing. The husband says she's on holiday and he's not worried. For his part, he's got a bit of goods along the road, but can't enjoy himself too openly because under the trust if he's caught out and divorced, he loses the cash. So until the eighteenth, he never stops very long with the woman, but on the eighteenth he stays the night and doesn't give a damn who sees the car." Murch swallowed the tablet. "All right. So where's the body?"

The divisional superintendent, a rotund man who was sharp on discipline yet who still managed to be on friendly terms with the men under him, stubbed out the cigarette he had been smoking. He looked at Jaeger.

"There's no sign of the body," said Jaeger.

"Have you looked for it?"

"Not yet, sir."

"Why not?"

"We've been finding out whether, or not, there's a body to look for. Until to-day, I haven't been a hundred per cent certain."

"And now you say you are, on evidence that isn't sufficient?"

Jaeger remained unruffled by the other's hostility. "Let's say I'm ninety-nine per cent certain, sir."

"She could still be alive. The husband might be right and she decided on a holiday. Or she might have been taken very ill—wasn't she suffering from something?"

"*Angina*, sir."

"That could have keeled her over."

"Quite, sir. But where's the body? And why wasn't she on the train that Leithan said he took her to catch?"

"What the hell's the use of asking me? You're supposed to be in charge."

"In that case, sir, we'll start looking for the body."

Murch stared at the map of the division which hung on the wall of the room. "Just what we bloody wanted. With everyone working flat out, one of my D.I.s presents me with a missing body so that I have to worry my ulcer nearer the grave." With a sweep of forgetfulness, he ignored the fact that only a few seconds ago he had disclaimed all responsibility in the affair.

: :   : :

Tuesday was market day in Ashford and on the twenty-seventh, as soon as all his duties for the morning were completed, Deakin prepared to go into town. He liked to study the low standards of other people's beasts, reinforce his poor opinion of other cowmen, buy a few vegetables from the Women's Institutes stall, and wander round and listen to the cheap-jacks as they sold shoddy goods to people less suspicious than he was.

He was about to walk away from the cow-sheds when he was hailed by a young man who quickly and officiously introduced himself as Detective-Constable Herald. Deakin took his ancient five-shilling watch from his pocket and consulted it.

"You've been working here a long time I wouldn't mind betting," said Herald.

"Wouldn't you," replied Deakin.

"Always for the old boy?"

"I've been with Mr. Leithan for twelve year."

"Is he a nice bloke to work for?"

"Why? Thinkin' of applying for a job?"

Herald's grin—his grin for gaffers, he called it— became a little strained. "I'll tell you something for free. I wouldn't spend my time mucking around with cows."

"I can reckon."

"What's Mrs. Leithan like?"

"Ain't so different to most women."

"Would you call her friendly to her husband?"

"Why don't you ask 'im?" Deakin consulted his watch again. "I've a bus to catch."

"You can hang on."

"It goes soon and I goes with it. And I've me best suit to put on yet."

"If you miss it, I'll run you into Ashford by car."

"Why?"

The interview had not gone as Herald had planned it. His voice became rougher. "You'll wait until I've finished asking you questions. I want to know if you've come across any disturbed earth?"

"What's that?"

"What's it sound like? Where someone's been digging."

"Folks is always digging." It was obvious that Deakin thought he was dealing with a fool.

"Have you come across any digging recently in any of the fields of this farm?"

"Why should I? I ain't been doin' it and no more's Alf."

"Someone else might have been."

"You'd better ask 'em, then."

"Look, Pop, let's get things clear. You'll give me a straight answer. Have you come across anywhere where there's been fresh digging?"

"Yes."

"Where?"

"My kitchen garden. Been preparing the clads for the frosties."

"I'm not asking you to be funny," shouted Herald.

Deakin looked at his watch again.

"Suppose I tell you, Pop, that if you don't answer me straight I'll run you into the police station and see what you've got to say for yourself there?"

"Then I'll tell you to booger off." Deakin replaced his watch. He looked at Josey who had calved a week before and he was glad to see that there were no signs of a return of the milk fever from which she had suffered. Then, he left.

: :   : :

Pamela drove to Lower Brakebourne Farm in the very ancient Morris that belonged to the two brothers who farmed the land beyond the woods in which her house was set. They lent it to her at threepence a mile. They were the kind of farmers who only barely made a living because they were so certain everything had to earn the greatest possible profit.

The Morris shuddered to a halt and Pamela climbed out. As she stared at the house, she remembered the last time she had been inside, and how she had felt so furious when Evadne had boasted that the old bricks, tiles, and wooden beams, meant absolutely nothing to her.

She drew the duffle coat more tightly about her, crossed to the front door and rang the bell. She heard the bubbling yowls of the Cuencas.

Mrs. Andrews opened the door and, with a warm smile, said that Mr. Leithan was working in the study. Pamela went through to that room. When she saw him, she was shocked by the lines in his face and the expression in his eyes. He put aside a book he had been reading and stood up. "Pamela . . ."

She closed the door. "If Charles Leithan won't go to Pamela, she must come to him. Where were you last night?" She tried to speak in a matter-of-fact voice. As she began to take off her duffle coat, he hurried forward to help her.

He put the coat down on the chair which stood immediately below the shelf in which were his ten published books. "I wasn't very well."

"You're a poor liar, Charles. I suppose it doesn't matter to you that I kept on expecting you right up until midnight? I was terrified something terrible had happened to you and I tried to phone, but they kept telling me your line was out of order."

He said nothing.

"Why didn't you come?"

"I . . . I've told you, I wasn't feeling very well. My head was giving me hell."

"And I've already told you that you make a damn' poor liar." She moved closer to him. "What were you doing?"

"Drinking," he muttered.

"You got so tight you couldn't drive?"

"No."

"Then why didn't you come?" She took hold of his right hand. "I was truly terrified something had happened to you."

He jerked his hand free and walked across to the window, then returned past her and went to the door that led directly into the sitting-room. He asked her to follow him and when they were in the other room he pointed at the window on the left-hand side of the far wall. "Have a look out there."

She did so. There was the garden as immaculate as ever, the far edge of the kennels that could just be seen beyond the evergreens which marked the end of the ornamental trees, the field, and the woods on the far side of the slope. A scene of quiet and peace and, to a country lover, a scene of beauty even in the middle of the death of winter. "Well?"

"Look at Coles Wood."

"I am."

"Can you see anyone in or around it?"

"No. But there are all those pigeons which are chasing around as if they're being disturbed."

"Ten policemen started searching in there yesterday afternoon. They were very polite about it, quite in the traditions of our wonderful British force. Would I mind very much if they just had a quick look. . . ." He turned away from the window, crossed to the corner cupboard and brought out a half-full bottle of whisky. He looked at her, but she shook her head. Sadly, she watched him pour himself a large whisky to which he added little soda. He drank eagerly. "I hope to God those brambles are ripping their legs to shreds."

"What if they are searching the woods?" she demanded.

"They're looking for her body."

"Obviously."

"They think I killed her."

"Equally obvious."

"Then what does that make me?"

"A possible murderer."

"You don't shrink from putting a name to it, do you?"

"I learned to be practical when Bernard died. Since then, I've never forgotten the lesson. If you call a spade a spade, Charles, no one can try to tell you it's a bloody shovel. We've both known what the police are thinking, but you've made the mistake of trying to ignore the fact."

"Have you come to sermonise?"

"Only to tell you that you won't change anything by drinking yourself silly."

"What's it matter? Why couldn't you stay at home?" Leithan, with the perverse anger that so often dogged him, finished his drink with ostentatious speed and helped himself to another.

She came across to him. "Are you going to do your very best to get rid of me? Has your very complicated mind decided that, as you're suspected of having murdered your wife, you mustn't remain friendly with me?"

He stared at her, unknowingly showing how much he needed her.

"You fool," she said softly. "Did you really think, in that confused mind of yours, that I'd remain at home and let you sweat it out all on your own?"

He wished he could explain, without any suggestion of heroics, that although her support was all that stood between him and a form of madness, when he had realised what such support could mean he had determined to do without it. There had, somehow, even been some satisfaction to be gained in the loneliness of that decision.

He put down his glass. "Pam. . . . Suppose they find her?"

"You'll need someone to hold your hand."

"But you . . ."

"I'm very good at holding hands—when they're yours."

He stared out of the window once more. This time, a figure was visible on the edge of Coles Wood.

CHAPTER X

WEDNESDAY, 12TH DECEMBER. It had been raining during most of the past two days and there seemed to be nothing dry left in the world.

Detective-Superintendent Murch looked almost as cheerless and washed out as the road outside the superintendent's room. "We say she's dead."

Jaeger looked at the uniformed superintendent and for a brief moment he thought he saw a quick wink. But the unlikelihood of the event convinced him he had been mistaken.

"She must be dead," continued Murch. "The evidence says so. I've checked it."

That's that, then, thought Jaeger.

"But what about proving it? Suppose we went to a court of law? What then? Shall I tell you? We'd be laughed out. When a man's tried for murder, you need a body. You, Jaeger, keep telling me it's murder. So where's the bloody body, eh?"

"Not on his farm, sir. I'll go nap on that."

"That's helpful. We now know the one place in the British Isles where it isn't. That takes us a long way, that does." He belched. "I said those potatoes would do me."

"Of course," remarked the divisional superintendent, "legally, there doesn't *have* to be a body."

"And we have enough evidence to present a case without one?" asked Murch belligerently.

"Not yet."

"Yet? That's a good word. Look, Bill, at the rate the thing's going, there never will be enough. Yet my D.I. doesn't seem to give a damn."

That was nonsense, as they all knew. The detective-inspector had left a number of jobs to Watters, jobs he should have been handling directly, in order to give as much time as possible to the Leithan case.

"The assistant chief constable was on to me about it."

"Did you ask him for more men?"

"No." Murch belched again. "Jesus, those potatoes!"

Jaeger knew what had to be done. It was a move no policeman willingly took, just in case the victim was an innocent party. But no one seriously considered Leithan to be innocent and he would have cracked before then, but for the woman. The D.I. had a genuine regard for Pamela Breslow. Underneath that charming exterior, she was as tough as they came: she had held Leithan upright when police pressure was threatening to knock him down. She disregarded everyone but the man she loved, and if her presence at Lower Brakebourne Farm made the neighbours talk more than ever, she did not give one solitary damn.

"I'll see what I can do," said Jaeger finally.

"Nothing stupid," warned Murch.

"Of course not, sir." The D.I. ironically thought that Murch was very quick to try to cover himself.

"Play it easily," said the divisional superintendent. He looked worried.

: :   : :

Just before midnight on the same day, Detective-Sergeant Watters entered the D.I.'s office and found the latter sprawled across his desk, asleep. "Wakey, wakey, rise and shine."

The D.I. raised his head and looked blearily at his sergeant. "Would you like to go and drown yourself?"

"No, sir, not until I've had my fill of my pension."

"What's the time?"

"Time to move."

Jaeger yawned and stood up. He had the beginnings

G

of a headache, no doubt caused by the dryness of air heated by an electric stove. "Who'd be a ruddy split?" He yawned again. "Any char going?"

"There's a cup on brew, sir."

"What's the night like?"

"As black as a buck nigger's belly and the wind's just called at the North Pole."

"Let's get something warm under our belts and then move. This time to-morrow, you and I may be able to spend all night in bed through being suspended from the force. Silly what we do sometimes, isn't it? Why do we?"

"Are you asking?"

"No. You'd only give me a bloody silly answer. But it's a question I've often pondered. Why do we make this more than a mere job? Suppose Leithan gets away with it—will you feel a terrible injustice has been done?"

"Not really."

"His wife was a bitch, from all accounts. If I had a bitch of a wife, I'd want to plant her out. Especially if Mrs. Breslow was waiting for me. He'd be a thousand times better off with her, but what happens? We're off to try and stop him getting away with something that ought to be his by right. Why?"

Watters was silent. He had lost interest both in the questions and the answers.

They went down to the ground floor and out of the station by the side door which brought them into the courtyard where the car was parked. They drove on to the road and at the end turned into Station Road. The wet, deserted streets lit from above had a kind of smeary impressionistic air about them.

They approached Lower Brakebourne Farm from the north and Jaeger parked the car at the edge of the orchard. He switched off the lights and the darkness covered them.

"We'll go close to the dogs," he said. "Unless they're even more stupid than they look, they'll kick up hell."

"What are they?"

"Look as if the cat's brought them in after a wet night, but they tell me they're very valuable."

They left the car and went along the road until they could climb a gate which brought them to the cinder path that led to the kennels. Soon, the bubbling yowling of the Cuencas began.

They reached the field below the garden. "You go down the slope," said the D.I., "and flash your torch around like mad."

Watters disappeared into the darkness and his progress was marked by the moving circle of light. Jaeger stared in the direction of the house.

A light went on in one of the upstairs rooms and the curtain seemed to move. Very soon Leithan would be out, demanding to know what was going on, burdened by a compulsive need to find out how much the police had discovered.

Leithan must break. He must say where he had buried the body of his wife. Guilt did very strange things. It turned strong men into weak ones, it made men talk when they knew their lives or their freedom depended on silence, it forced them into action when they were certain safety lay in inaction.

Leithan must break. Jaeger flashed his torch so that the beam was clearly visible from the house.

CHAPTER XI

Within easy reach of the Ashford-Canterbury road were a number of woods of varying sizes. Many of them provided playgrounds of irresistible charm to the local children. Cowboys and Indians was a very exciting game when played in woods that were keepered, since all keepers were known to be cannibals.

Patrick, by two years the junior, followed where Raymond led—even when this meant going into Frog Wood. Ostensibly, they were looking for dead pheasants which might have been shot and not picked up on the previous Saturday. Pheasants were said to be worth ten shillings each.

Slowly, carefully, and frightened, they made their way into Frog Wood—it formed the first part of Roman Woods—and soon came to a small, shallow pond on which they saw two moorhens. They were uncertain whether these were worth ten shillings each. Raymond recalled a television programme in which natives put earthenware jars over their heads and drifted down on to ducks which were pulled under water by their feet, but rather to the relief of the boys it was obvious that the pond was far too shallow for any such operation.

They continued on their way and came to a ride which led back to the road. They turned down it and were hurrying towards the road, satisfied they had been in the enemy's territory long enough to prove their courage, when Raymond saw a bundle of he knew not quite what. He went up to it. There was hair, bones, and what looked like an eye. He told Patrick to come closer. Patrick reluctantly did so. He found a leather collar with a metal plate on it on which was written Stymphalian of

Saavedra, and a telephone number. There was also a metal disc with an address on one side and a promise on the other to pay five shillings to the finder.

: :   : :

Jaeger stood in the main ride of Frog Wood and stared down at what remained of the dog's head and neck. Strangely, he found himself pitying the poor beast.

He spoke to Yelt, the keeper, a tall and gangling man with a floppy moustache. "Does it say anything to you?"

The keeper shook his head.

Jaeger spoke in a friendly voice. "Look, it's important. So if you killed it because it was worrying your pheasants, tell me, and I promise it won't go any further. But I must know."

Yelt spoke scornfully. "If I found a dog what was up with the birds, you wouldn't see it again and no more would anyone else."

Jaeger smiled. "All right. Any idea, then, where it's come from?"

"None."

"I take it you know these woods pretty well?"

"I reckon." Yelt opened his gun and checked that it was empty. He laid the gun on the ground and rolled himself a cigarette. "Better'n anyone else, but that don't mean I guarantee every inch. There's two hundred acres back in Roman Woods and some of 'em is proper jungle."

"Keeping all that in mind, where d'you suggest we start searching for the rest of the dog?"

Yelt pushed his cap to the back of his head. He stared with hate up through the trees at a passing crow. "You know what I reckon?"

"You tell me."

"I'd say the old vixen knows the answer. I say the dog was shot and left lying round, and that the old vixen what I've been layin' for for the last month had a good eat."

Jaeger tapped the bowl of his pipe on the heel of his right shoe. "You've just said you didn't shoot it."

"No more I did. But if it ain't been shot, I'll quit keeperin'. Seen the skull?"

"Not close to."

"I always looks at the deads to see what killed 'em. If it's a fox, stoat, weasel, cat, owl, or crow, I wants to know. That dog's skull's smashed, and I don't reckon nothing but a gun did it."

Jaegar separated the stem of his pipe from the bowl and blew it clear. He rejoined the two, filled the bowl with tobacco. "Thanks." He turned and walked back twenty feet to where Watters and Herald were waiting. "The dog was probably shot."

"What kind of gun, sir?"

Jaeger shrugged his shoulders. "What guns has Leithan?"

They looked blankly at him. He swore. "Haven't any of you checked?"

Secure in the knowledge that in the final analysis the blame for not having checked was his, they remained silent.

"Herald, go and find out. Watters, phone the super-intendent and warn him we may have to search the woods." He lit his pipe with the first match. Because Pamela Breslow stood squarely behind Leithan, Leithan hadn't cracked. But maybe it would no longer be necessary to try to wear him down, to crowd suspicion on top of fear until the load became too heavy. Maybe they had found the burial ground.

: :   : :

Leithan walked into the dining-room and found Pamela already sitting down. "Sorry I'm late." He had told her what the police were doing to him at night-time, and she had reacted in typical manner. Ignoring everyone, including him, she practically moved into Lower Brakebourne Farm.

She pressed the bell under the carpet that would tell Mrs. Andrews to start serving. "Were you carried away by your own eloquence?" She studied his face and noted that it was a little less strained than it had been.

"I was trying to reach the end of a chapter," he replied, as he sat down.

"I read those two chapters you gave me, Charles."

"And?"

"You've made it," Her lie went undetected. She saw the quick expression of pleasure cross his face.

Mrs. Andrews entered with a tray on which were two plates of potted shrimps. "Don't be long, Mr. Leithan, the pheasant'll be cooked to a turn in five minutes," she said, as she served them.

"Right."

Mrs. Andrews made certain the slices of lemon and the pepper mill were there, then she left the room.

Pamela helped herself to lemon and a trace of pepper. "I meant that, Charles. The book is really something new."

"Wouldn't it be odd if I proved you right after all?"

"Not in the slightest."

"You always said I ought to meet some of the muck of life and turn myself into a second Dostoyevsky." He had not spoken as lightly as he had meant. The muck of life might have helped his writing but it stank, and immortality was a pretty useless commodity to the mortal.

They finished the shrimps and the pheasant was brought in. Mrs. Andrews, self-taught, was an excellent cook. The pheasant was sweet and succulent, the roast potatoes were crisp, and even though the green peas had been deep frozen she had provided them with taste.

Following the pheasant came a very "tipsy" trifle, topped with an inch of honest Jersey cream.

They went through to the sitting-room. "Cognac?" asked Leithan.

She hesitated. "A small one, then, Charles." She had managed to persuade him to cut down his drinking.

He poured out two cognacs and handed her a glass as Mrs. Andrews brought in the coffee. At that moment, there was the sound of a car door as it was slammed shut and all three turned and looked through the north window. They saw Herald as he walked up to the front door.

Leithan drank quickly. "Can't they ever leave a man alone?"

"You must complain," snapped Pamela.

Mrs. Andrews left the room. Her thoughts on the subject that was so intriguing the villagers were quite clear. Mr. Leithan might have "removed" Mrs. Leithan, but if so, she was neither concerned nor surprised. Wasn't he an author?

"You must complain," said Pamela, for the second time. From the way he nodded his head, she knew he would not.

Herald appeared. "'Afternoon," he said loudly.

Leithan opened the large silver cigarette box and offered it to Pamela, then to Herald. Herald shook his head. "I prefer to keep my wind."

"For the porridge?" asked Pamela.

The quotation escaped the detective. "Can't stand the stuff." He turned. "Have you got any guns, Mr. Leithan?"

Leithan replaced the cigarette box on the small tripod table. "Why?"

"Just a check."

"A check for what?" demanded Pamela.

Herald turned to her and was angrily reminded that she had complained of the way he had looked at her. "It's a general one."

"Can't you answer the question?" Her voice was quietly contemptuous.

Herald shrugged his broad shoulders.

Leithan hastened to answer the original question and so forestall anything more Pamela might say. "I've a pair of Churchills and a two-two."

"What are they?" Herald was annoyed he had to ask.

"The Churchills are shotguns, the two-two is a vermin rifle."

"Can I see 'em, please, and your licence."

Leithan left the room. Herald stared at the bottle of cognac and wondered if he would be offered a drink, but when he saw the expression on Pamela Breslow's face he knew that the only thing she would willingly give him would be prussic acid.

Leithan returned with a firearm certificate and a rifle equipped with telescopic sights. "I'll get the guns," he said and left again.

Herald opened the certificate and found it listed ten weapons.

Leithan brought two leather cases into the room. He put them on the floor and opened them.

Herald only gave the shotguns a cursory glance. "The licence says you've nine pistols as well as that rifle?"

"They are hanging in the hall. Some old pistols need a licence, some don't, and I've never really been able to find the dividing line."

Herald read through the list again. "Is the Webley out there?"

"The four fifty-five? That's in my bedroom."

"I'd like to see it, please."

Leithan went out, after closing the shotgun cases.

Pamela stubbed out the cigarette she had been smoking. She finished her brandy.

"It's cold outside, but more than hot enough in here," said Herald.

"That's because the central heating's on."

You bitch, thought Herald, but how snooty will you be when you learn the dog's been found? He took a sweet from his pocket, unwrapped it, and put it into his mouth. "Not a bad little house, this."

"I'm glad you commend it."

"Look, lady, I'm not here because I want to be. I was sent."

"Your explanation, of course, makes your presence welcome."

He wished he dared be rude back, but that would probably cost him his job.

Pamela tried to hear the sound of footsteps on the stairs. There was silence. Why hadn't Charles returned with the revolver? It had belonged to his uncle and was kept in his chest of drawers in his bedroom: a minute should have been more than enough in which to fetch it. She poured herself another brandy.

Herald looked at his watch again. "Would you think he's having trouble?"

She desperately willed Charles to hurry up.

Despite himself, Herald spoke again and even he realised his words had been foolish. "There's one thing, I couldn't stand living in a house this warm."

She ignored him. Shortly afterwards, they heard Leithan come down the stairs. He entered the room and there was no mistaking the expression on his face. Pamela looked down at his empty hands.

"I can't understand it. It isn't there."

"No, sir?" said Herald.

"The holster's empty. I keep it in a drawer I don't normally use and . . ."

Herald rudely interrupted. "Have you any ammunition for it?"

"I . . . I'm not allowed any. If you look at the certificate . . ."

"I have, and I'm not asking what's official. How many rounds have you?"

Leithan lit a cigarette.

"How many rounds have you, sir?"

"Just a few. I . . . I was given some years ago and I've always kept them. They could be useful for self-defence, even if I couldn't hit a barn door at five paces."

"I'd like to see them, please."

Leithan brought down ten squat, lead-nosed cartridges which had patches of green verdigris on the brass cases.

"Is that all there should be?"

"Yes."

But the detective had not missed the hesitation. "I'll take them, please." He stood up and held out his hand. "Would you like a receipt?"

"Yes," said Pamela.

Angrily, Herald wrote out a receipt for ten ·455 cartridges. "Let us know when you find the gun, won't you?" he said, and only just managed to contain his sarcasm.

Herald left the house, and through the window they watched him climb into the battered Austin and drive away.

"The gun's vanished," said Leithan hoarsely. "It was there the last time I looked, I know it was. And some of the cartridges have gone."

She shut her eyes for a brief moment. "Are you sure?"

"Of course I am."

"You haven't moved it anywhere and forgotten about it?"

"I never handle it, from one end of the year to the next. Why the hell should I?" The anger in his voice, which was plainly no more than fear, died away. He crossed to the chair in which Pamela was sitting.

She took his hand in hers and held on to it with the force of desperation. "Go and see Phil."

"Why?"

"Please promise me you'll go and see him right away."

"But . . ."

"No buts."

He looked down and saw that her eyes were filled with tears. "All right," he said, and in his voice there was no hope.

: :   : :

Phillimore Enty was full of obvious bonhomie. There was a cheerful touch of vulgarity about him that suggested the convivial temperament of a man who enjoyed the brassier sides of life. "Well, Charles, what's the panic you mentioned?" He sat down behind his large desk.

"Evadne." Leithan felt like a sick man going to his doctor in search of a miracle cure in which he could not believe.

Enty's manner became more restrained. "I can't say I'm surprised. The police were here, asking about your financial status. I gave them the terms of your father's will, since they can find that out any day of the week, but naturally refused them anything else."

"They . . . they think I've killed her."

Enty began to drum on his desk with his fingers.

"Phil, God knows what's going to happen so I want to make certain Pamela Breslow doesn't suffer too long. Will you draw up a new will for me, leaving her everything? After that, start worrying about me."

"When you say everything, are you including the trust money?"

"Of course. If Evadne is . . . dead, the capital's automatically mine."

The rate at which Enty's fingers drummed the desk increased. "I wish it were that easy, Charles—I mean the question of the money—but it isn't. One of the rules of inheritance is that a man can't make capital out of his crime and inherit under the will of a person whose death he caused by murder or manslaughter. By analogy, if the very worst comes to the worst, and it's proved Evadne is dead and you are somehow found responsible, it's unlikely you'd be allowed to take the capital of the trust."

Leithan briefly closed his eyes. Until now, there had been one ray of light in the middle of the filthy mess: Pam would be financially all right. But now he could no longer even enjoy that sense of relief. He knew she had not been writing as much as she should have been, so that her work was behind schedule and at least one of her editors had complained, but it had not mattered. With the trust fund behind her, she would never again need to worry about money. But now . . . "She's got to have it. You must find a way."

Enty stopped drumming and moved his hand off the top of the desk. "I'll try," he said, and the tone of his voice said the attempt was hopeless.

Leithan hated his wife more than ever.

CHAPTER XII

Roman Woods had the shape of a very disproportionate figure eight. The top circle, Frog Wood, was twenty acres in size, while the bottom circle was 200 acres. Since the head of the dog had been found in Frog Wood, the police began their search there, and those who could appreciate the size and density of Roman Woods hoped there would be no need to go farther. At the same time as the first policeman reluctantly began walking through the wood, the skull of Stymphalian was examined by a vet and a pathologist. They were both agreed that the dog had probably been killed by a heavy calibre bullet fired at very close range.

At Ashford police station, the D.I. paced up and down his room and thought about Detective-Superintendent Murch who was yelling for action. Murch was good at yelling for action, but bad at helping to provide it.

The telephone rang and he crossed to the desk and lifted the receiver. "D.I. speaking."

"Watters, sir. We've found the rest of the dog by a small hole that was almost certainly meant to be its grave."

"Have you learned anything more?"

"I haven't investigated very closely, sir. I thought you'd rather we kept clear: that leaves you to make all the mistakes."

"I'll be out." Jaeger replaced the receiver. After a couple of minutes' thought, he went down to the divisional superintendent's office and reported the latest development. He then left a message for the photographer to go to Roman Woods, after which he went out to his car.

He thought of all the work that was piling up on his desk and sighed heavily: no matter how rushed a D.I. might be, H.Q. always wanted the paper work to be carefully attended to.

He drove rapidly along the Canterbury road until he came to the row of cars, parked on the grass verge. He climbed out of his car and went into Frog Wood. Immediately, the thick wet clay began to ball up on his shoes and he cursed himself for being so stupid as to forget wellingtons.

Watters was waiting on the ride and he led Jaeger through the tall and whippy fifteen-year growth of chestnut, elm, hornbeam, and oak, to a small pit about two feet deep, the bottom of which was filled with water. To the right of the pit was the battered and headless body of a dog.

The D.I. studied the area and he noted a patch of brambles which had been flattened in the centre. The brambles lay between the pit and the road. "Have you had a close look at that lot?"

Watters shook his head. "I've held everyone back, sir."

Jaeger went over and stood in the brambles, close to the flattened strip. A body, dragged through them, would leave such a mark. He bent down and looked closely at the separate vines, with their long curved thorns, and on one he saw several hairs.

He stood up and went back to where Watters was waiting. "One of those brambles has hairs on it. We'll photograph the hairs and then send 'em to the lab at the same time as the dog. If the bullet isn't in the dog we can start looking for that. In the meantime, start an intensive search round here, using that hole as the centre. Call the men in and re-deploy them, and tell 'em if they put their big feet down on anything important I'll bloody well skin them."

"Yes, sir."

Jaeger took his pipe from his pocket and rubbed his cheek with the bowl. The cold wet wind flapped the collar of his mackintosh against his neck. "Shot here and dragged to the road."

"Looks that way, sir."

The searching policemen were ordered to begin their new task, spreading outwards in an ever-enlarging circle. Soon, there was a call from beyond the brambles in which the hairs had been found. Jaeger went across and was shown a suitcase and a handbag, which were some five feet apart.

He opened the handbag and was immediately conscious of the smell of scent. Inside, were the usual things a woman carried round with her, plus a small diary in the front of which were Evadne Leithan's name and her address. He turned his attention to the suitcase. It was a large pigskin one with the intitials E.L. in gold on the top. He searched it. There were pyjamas, silk dressing-gown, slippers, a set of underclothes, a dress, a sweater, and a sponge-bag. These articles had only filled a quarter of the space and had been held in position by the interior straps. He pulled out the pyjamas which lay on top and he noted the dog's hairs all over them and felt irritation at people who treated dogs so unnaturally as to take them to bed.

There was a second call which took him back to the hole. Close by it, previously covered by dead leaves, was a revolver. Almost certainly, it was a .455 Webley. No one could say he was surprised.

The detective-constable who was the police photographer came into sight and the D.I. ordered him to photograph the revolver first. When that had been done, the D.I. put on a pair of plastic gloves, picked up the revolver, and examined it. There was little chance of finding fingerprints on it, but nevertheless all possible precautions to preserve them, should there be any, had to be taken. He broke the gun. There were three cartridges in the cylinder, two of which had been fired. He dropped the gun into a plastic bag.

The photographer took the last of the shots of the remains of the dog and Watters ordered Leery to bag up the corpse. Very reluctantly, Leery began his task.

The search continued, slowly spreading outwards.

: :   : :

The gun was tested for fingerprints and, as expected, none was found. The hairs, taken from the brambles, were sent to the laboratories at New Scotland Yard and by the middle of the next morning a report on them was telephoned to Kent. The hairs were human, probably from a female whose age lay between early adult and late middle-age. If comparison hairs could be obtained, it might be possible to gain a positive identification.

By 11.15 a.m. it was certain that Evadne Leithan had not been buried between the spot where the dog had been found and the road, or within three hundred yards in the opposite direction. The searching policemen, made more miserable than ever by a light drizzle, thought that in view of the evidence this would now be the end of their labours. But their hopes came to nothing when they were told that because no bullet had been found in the dog's body, they were going to have to dig all round the hole to try to recover it. Also, a search of the rest of Frog Wood must be made.

At 3.27 p.m., a slightly misshapen lead bullet was recovered from the middle of a spadeful of thick yellow clay. It was handed to Watters who dropped it into a plastic bag.

: :   : :

The following morning, the 19th December, a constable

H

was walking in Frog Wood close to where the handbag had been found and his foot kicked into something. This proved to be a small chemist's bottle. How the bottle had been missed before was something of a mystery, a mystery Jaeger preferred to call bloody incompetence.

The D.I. looked at the label which was still attached. Rain had washed whatever writing had been on it, but had not obliterated the name of an Ashford chemist. He unscrewed the top and rolled into the palm of his hand two of the tablets from inside. He wondered what they were, never before having seen any in that strange greyish colour. He replaced them in the bottle and called Herald over. "Get this to the station and have it checked for prints. Then send it to the lab and ask 'em if they can bring out on the label whatever was written on it. Once you've organised that, take one of the pills along to the chemist and have it identified."

Herald did not try to hide his pleasure at being able to escape from the dark, dripping, clay-bound woods.

: :   : :

Six test bullets were fired from the .455 Webley, found in Frog Wood, into a long steel box which was packed tight with cotton-wool. The six bullets were then recovered. The incriminating bullet—the one taken from the clay in the wood—was, together with one of the test bullets, fitted into a comparison microscope which merged the two images into one by means of the eyepiece. This experiment, as expected, gave a positive identification and photographs were taken.

: :   : :

A scientist carefully placed the label, removed from the chemist's bottle, on to a sheet of plain cardboard and photographed it under ultra-violet light. This failed to bring up the washed-out writing. He placed ammonium sulphide in a dish in a cupboard and added hydrochloric

acid, rested the cardboard above the dish so that the
fumes played on it, and shut the front of the cupboard.
He lit a cigarette.

Twenty-five minutes later, brown writing appeared on
the label and it was photographed before it had time to
disappear again.

"Mrs. Leithan. Take one tablet, to be crushed in
mouth, as required."

: :   : :

Murch muttered something about his ulcer and became
even more morose when he was not offered any sympathy;
Jaeger fidgeted with his pipe; the uniformed superintendent signed his name to some of the many reports
that had to be sent to H.Q. There was a knock on the
door and a police cadet showed a man wearing black
coat and striped trousers into the room.

"Good morning," said the newcomer.

"'Morning, Mr. Turkaine," replied the uniformed
superintendent. "Still peddling law?"

Turkaine, a very solemn member of the D.P.P.'s
office, looked annoyed. He sat down in the empty
chair, opened his brief-case and brought out a folder in
which were a number of papers neatly tied in white tape.
He coughed. "This is an unusual case, of course, since
the body of the deceased has not yet been recovered. It
would make things very much easier if you could find
it."

Jaeger spoke. "We've searched the place dry."

"Quite so. But I tell you perfectly frankly, a murder
case without a body is a very tricky affair. Very tricky."
Turkaine looked round and his prim features suggested a
certain delight at the professional complexity of the case.
"The law in the matter, you must understand . . ."

"Just before we go into that, sir," broke in Jaeger,
"I wonder if you'd answer a question?"

"What?"

"With the evidence we now have, do you think a case can be brought if one bears in mind the fact that it's obvious, because of the position of the hair in relation to the dog, that the dead woman was dragged to the road and removed in a car?"

"I was obviously intending to deal fully with that question later on, but since you've brought it up I suppose I might as well answer it now. There are no facts which will prove that the body was dragged to the road."

"No, sir, but since the hair . . ."

"I mentioned facts, Inspector. You must not forget that we have to present the jury either with facts that speak for themselves or else with circumstantial evidence so strong they must accept it. You and I may be satisfied that the missing bullet is in the dead woman, that she was dragged to the road and there loaded into a car and taken somewhere else to be buried by a man who was being so careful that he would not leave the body in the same place as the dog—but we have to prove this to the jury. Therefore we must search the woods for the negative evidence of the absence of a grave or a body."

"But we have searched Frog Wood, sir."

"You must include Roman Woods." Turkaine held up his hand. "I've read the report and know perfectly well the size of these woods and how closely they resemble a jungle, also that the keeper has reported nothing. To this, my reply is first, that the keeper knew nothing about the dead dog, the hole, the handbag and the suitcase, so obviously his evidence is not sufficiently reliable, and secondly, no matter how dense the woods, the search must be made—including, let it be clearly understood, the three lakes. They must be dragged. We must forestall an obvious line of attack of the defence."

"What about all the other woods in the district?" said the D.I. with mild sarcasm.

"I doubt whether I need ask you to go through all of them as well. I rather imagine the jury will be sufficiently impressed by the evidence you will be presenting, regarding the tremendous effort involved in overcoming the hazards of nature to be found in Roman Woods."

The D.I. was surprised to discover that the other was human enough to return the sarcasm.

"Now, as to the legal position." Turkaine, unaware of what he was doing, rubbed his hands together. "In the case of Regina and Onufrejczyk, it was held . . ."

: :   : :

The police searched Roman Woods. They forced their way through acres of dead bracken and brambles, through rhododendron bushes that had spread so thickly they were almost impenetrable, and they dragged the three lakes. As they could have told the D.P.P.'s office from the very beginning, they found nothing. But then, being civil servants, the D.P.P. men wanted two dots to every i and two crosses to every t.

: :   : :

Leithan had, back in September, been invited to a shoot on the Saturday before Christmas. On the Friday evening, he telephoned to say he was afraid he could not turn up. He thought he heard relief in the other man's voice. He was not surprised. By now, it was generally known in the district that he was suspected of having murdered his wife.

On the Saturday morning, Pamela returned from Ashford at twelve-fifteen. She had had her hair trimmed and was wearing a new dress. As Leithan told her, just before he kissed her, she looked very beautiful.

She smiled. "Sometimes, Charles, you almost become romantic."

"And what's the word 'almost' doing there?"

"It's explaining that, with typical male arrogance, you're already taking me for granted. I'm no longer a mistress to be flattered, only a housewife to be cursed if things aren't run efficiently."

"You're an idiot."

"Thank you for those few kind words, which explain everything so much more clearly than ever I could have done."

He tickled her and, as always, she soon had to call for peace. "If you carry on," she gasped, "I won't give you your pre-Christmas present."

He stopped and kissed her. "Where and what?"

"In the car."

Arm-in-arm they went over to the Rapier. On the back seat were a number of packages, one of which was obviously a magnum-sized bottle. He picked it up.

"Trust you to recognise it if it's drink!"

He began to shiver from the contrast between the temperature outside and inside and hurriedly carried the shopping basket and the bottle into the house.

Back in the sitting-room, he tore off the brown paper covering the bottle. "Heidsieck, forty-seven. The girl has taste. Where are the nearest glasses?"

"Just you and I can't drink it."

"What's the use of a present if it doesn't lead to dissipation. If only I can make you sufficiently giggly..." He whispered in her ear and she called him a dirty old man.

He felt the bottle to decide whether it needed chilling and gladly decided the day had already sufficiently done that. He went through to the kitchen and returned with three tall, fluted, champagne glasses—Mrs. Andrews had to be offered a little.

He opened the bottle and poured out three glassfuls and Mrs. Andrews entered the room and drank with a speed and determination that might have suggested she was having to take medicine. When the glass was empty she returned to the kitchen.

"Here's to us," said Leithan, as he refilled his glass.

"To us, Charles. Maybe the luck will begin to run with us now."

With harsh irony, the police car arrived as she finished speaking. They watched Jaeger and Watters climb out.

Leithan drained his glass and for him, all the bubbles had disappeared.

The detectives were shown into the room by an openly indignant Mrs. Andrews, who slammed the door shut as she left.

Jaeger spoke quietly. "Charles Leithan, I am arresting you for the murder of your wife, Evadne Leithan. I intend to take you to Ashford police station where you will be charged. Neither here nor there are you obliged to say anything, but anything you say will be taken down and may be used in evidence."

"It's . . ." Pamela choked and became silent.

"We found the dog," said Jaeger, not unkindly.

"Dog?" muttered Leithan.

"It had been shot with your revolver."

"Stymie?"

"It was a Cuenca."

"That's ridiculous. She can't have been shot. Stymie can't have been shot," repeated Leithan wildly.

CHAPTER XIII

LEITHAN WAS ESCORTED up the stairs and into the dock which stood in the centre of the assize court. As he encountered the gaze of so many, he instinctively retreated a step. The policeman behind him seemed to think he was going to panic and murmured: "Take it easy."

Events blurred together and the next positive event of which he was aware was when he heard his name. He forced himself to concentrate and saw that Enty and Tarnton were standing by the side of the dock.

"Charles, Mr. Tarnton wants a word with you before the judge comes in," said Enty.

"Yes?"

Tarnton was one of the few Q.C.s whose name was very widely known to the public. "Have you been able to remember anything which will help to show ill-will on the part of the Pochard girl?" He had an angular face, with a pointed nose and upturned chin. His eyes were a very light blue, so blue that even behind his spectacles they were his most noticeable feature.

Leithan tried to forget all the people who were staring at him. "Sarah Pochard hardly stayed long enough to show either good- or ill-will. The only thing I can remember is that I had to tell her to get on with the work once or twice."

Tarnton rested his proof on the edge of the dock and wrote in the margin of it. "Can you give me definite occasions and the words used?"

"No, I can't."

"Was she slack?"

"Completely."

"D'you remember her evidence at the preliminary

hearing regarding the row between you and your wife?"

"Vaguely."

"You'll have to remember better than vaguely, Mr. Leithan, for everybody's sake. How much of what she said was accurate?"

Leithan desperately tried to think back. "I can't swear any of it's inaccurate."

"Pity. Now, what about the revolver?"

"The last time I saw it, it was in the usual drawer. Look, I couldn't have shot Stymie. I couldn't have shot her."

Tarnton raised his eyebrows that were still black and in sharp contrast to such of his silver hair as was visible beneath his somewhat dirty wig. "I suggest you concentrate more on the unlikelihood of your having shot your wife," he said dryly.

"For God's sake, Charles," said Enty, "forget the dog. Remember that the jury might misunderstand what you're saying. And try to look and sound as if you're fighting the charge."

Wearily, Leithan supposed they were right. They were the experts.

The usher called for silence, the red-robed judge came through the open doorway on to the dais and, just before he sat down, bowed in return to the bows of counsel. Mr. Justice Cator had an unusual looking face—one counsel, who had reason to dislike him, always said he looked like a rather tired marmoset.

Tarnton and Enty went to their benches. Leithan was called to the bar and the indictment was read out: his plea of not guilty was taken: the jury were called and sworn.

Alliter, Q.C., prepared to open the case.

: :   : :

". . . Members of the jury," said Alliter, soon after he had begun to speak, "I feel I should outline the law concerning murder when there is no body of the deceased."

"Mr. Alliter," said the judge, and his voice was very deep for a small man, "I shall naturally be dealing with that point at some length myself."

"Quite so, my Lord, but I feel the jury should appreciate the law before we go too deeply into the facts."

"Very well." The judge leaned back in his chair in a resigned manner.

"Members of the jury," repeated Alliter, "as you know, the prisoner is charged with the murder of his wife, the body of whom has not been recovered. Although such proceedings are unusual, they are certainly not unique and the law in the matter is quite clear.

"Many of you will have heard the expression *corpus delicti*. Contrary to popular belief, this does not refer to the body. What it does mean is that a crime has been committed; or, to put it in another way, that the person to whom the charges relate is dead and that the person's death has been caused by a crime.

"The fact of death can be proved in two ways. Directly, by medical examination of a body by a competent physician who pronounces life to be extinct, or circumstantially, which means a case where all the circumstances point to one conclusion—the death—and cannot point to another, and in which there is no shadow of doubt in any mind that the person must be dead.

"The burden of proving everything in this trial is on the Crown: which means that, for a verdict of guilty, if there were no answer from the prisoner at the end of the case for the prosecution, you would be certain that the prosecution's contentions were right. If, however, you are not so satisfied, there is no need for the prisoner—in order to clear your minds—to answer any of the queries that have been raised; there is absolutely no burden on him."

Alliter looked at the judge and the expression on his lean face was a trifle sardonic. "I trust, my Lord, you approve?"

"I found nothing, Mr. Alliter, of which I could specifically disapprove."

Alliter continued speaking to the jury. "Those are some of the points you must constantly bear in mind. You have to be satisfied that the prosecution makes it one hundred per cent clear that there can be no explanation for the known and proved facts other than that Evadne Leithan is dead, that she was murdered—and you will note that although we say she was shot, this is not a case of capital murder—and that the prisoner, Charles Leithan, murdered her.

"What are these facts? What has taken place to make it quite certain. . . ."

: :   : :

The first witness to be called was the ticket-collector. He had put on his Sunday suit and was enjoying his appearance in court.

After the preliminary questions had been put and answered, Alliter, noted in many Bar messes as a vocal vegetarian, said: "Were you on duty at the gates of the up platform of Ashford station on Sunday, 18th November?"

"I was."

"Were you there between ten and twelve-thirty?"

"Yes, sir."

"All the time?"

"Without a single break."

"How can you be so certain?"

"I know that day, I do. It was when there was all that fog and the trains was running late."

"Do you know Mrs. Leithan?"

"Not much, I don't. I was bitten by one of her dogs,

and when I accidentally kicked it, like, she went and reported me. Didn't do no good, though," he added, with satisfaction.

"Did you see Mrs. Leithan between the hours of ten and twelve-thirty on Sunday, 18th November, last year?"

"No."

Alliter sat down. Tarnton stood up and smiled pleasantly. "I suppose you're certain you know Mrs. Leithan by sight?"

"Not much, I ain't."

"Tell me, how many travellers do you see each day?" Tarnton's voice was calm and musical and it possessed the rare quality that it was interesting to listen to, no matter what he was saying.

"I don't know. Thousands, maybe."

"I suppose you wouldn't claim to recognise all of them?"

"Most of 'em. I've a mind for faces. They kind of stick in me memory. Many's the time I've said to the missus . . ."

"Knowing so many faces, you might, of course, easily confuse one with another?"

"What d'you mean?"

"You might recognise A on the eleven o'clock, B on the twelve o'clock, and inadvertently switch them around in your mind?"

"I don't get it."

Patiently, Tarnton simplified his question and then continued with the cross-examination. It was not long before he brought it to a close. The witness was certain that Mrs. Leithan had not travelled on the eleven forty-two and nothing would shake his certainty. Tarnton had been pretty sure that that was how it would be, but this was one of the rare trials in which it would be safe thoroughly to cross-examine some witnesses even though their stories were quite definite and unlikely to be seriously shaken. In the absence of a body, the jury were not going to want to convict and the slightest breach of the prosecution's case might swing them over; whilst, by the same reasoning, lack of effectiveness of cross-examination would not hinder the defence.

Alan Marsh, too smart, too sleek, took the oath. He testified that he and his wife had driven to Charing Cross station to meet the train on which they had been told by Mrs. Leithan she would arrive, and that she had not been on it. He had telephoned the prisoner to try to find out what had happened and although Leithan had at first seemed worried, later it became clear that he was not concerned by his wife's non-appearance and had even angrily refused any suggestion that they should try to find out if anything were wrong. He, Marsh, and his wife had continued to expect Mrs. Leithan to arrive, but they had never seen her again. She had even not attended the A.G.M., though it was certain she would have attended it if humanly possible. He had not heard a word from her from that day to this.

Tarnton rose and cross-examined. "Let's look more closely at the telephone call you made on the eighteenth, Mr. Marsh. You got through to Kent to say that Mrs. Leithan had not arrived on the train?"

"That's it, only we waited until the next one was in and she weren't on that either, and we got home before we phoned."

"And you claim the accused did not seem to treat the matter as being of importance?"

"I said I couldn't understand how he was so calm about it, not wanting to call in the police nor anyone else. He even got angry with me for suggesting it."

"You find that beyond your comprehension?"

"If my wife caught a train she didn't arrive on, I'd worry, I know that."

"But this does not concern either your wife, or you."

Tarnton's voice became slightly sarcastic. "There are some people in this world, Mr. Marsh, who do not parade their feelings on their coat sleeves."

"Yes, but . . ."

"But what?"

"He just weren't worried."

"You really can't say that. The most you can say is that, in so far as you were able to judge—which obviously wasn't very far—the man at the other end of the telephone line did not sound worried. But this means your evidence is valueless, doesn't it? The accused might have been beside himself with worry and you obviously wouldn't have known anything about it, since all that struck you was the fact that his voice remained calm?"

"But if my wife . . ."

"Is your wife missing, Mr. Marsh?"

"Of course she isn't."

"Then shall we leave the sad subject of your feelings on her disappearance until that painful event actually takes place?" Tarnton was glad to see a quick smile on the face of the man at the end of the front row in the jury box. "Mr. Marsh, you have testified that you were certain Mrs. Leithan would attend the annual general meeting of the Cuenca Club. Why are you so positive?"

"I've already said as it was the decision on tri-colours. She'd done everything possible to make certain the vote went her way; and she knew that to win, all she had to do was to turn up."

"Would you be a little more explicit about precisely how she had done everything possible?"

Marsh hesitated. "Spoken to people, and so on."

"What do you mean by 'so on'?"

"She gave a cocktail party."

"Was that all?"

"Well . . ."

"Well, what?"

"She offered to pay the expenses of people who had to travel a distance to get to the meeting."

"Just their travelling expenses?"

"There was a question of meals . . ."

"Shall we call it bribery?"

Marsh flushed. "It wasn't bribing . . ." He did not finish the sentence.

Tarnton allowed the silence to continue for several seconds. "Not quite cricket," he finally commented sardonically.

Marsh shifted his weight from one foot to the other and found great difficulty in knowing what to do with his hands.

"Don't you think, Mr. Marsh, that a woman who is normally scrupulously honest, but who in a moment of weakness departs from such standards, might suddenly regret all she had done and would determine to right the wrong? That she would make certain her scheme should not be further implemented?"

"She didn't think like that."

"You don't really like Mrs. Leithan, do you?"

"We was very great friends."

"Are you quite certain?"

"Yes."

"Yet *you* are not friendly enough to admit that she might have had a change of heart for the better?"

"She wanted to get her dog made up a champion," said Marsh, with brash loudness. "There wasn't anything in the world would have kept her away from the meeting."

"That is, in your opinion. The opinion of a man who found that all his unpopular spade-work had been wasted." Tarnton sat down. Farmen, his junior, leaned forward.

"Stubborn bastard," said Farmen.

"Wouldn't you be, if you were telling the truth?"

Judy Marsh took the oath. When she had finished, she reached up and fiddled with her hair at the back of her head. She had done everything possible to make herself smart and had committed all the faults of a woman without any natural taste.

Alliter began his examination. "Were you expecting a visitor to your house on the 18th November?"

"Mrs. Leithan, Evadne, was coming to stay with us. She quite often used to spend time with us." For one brief moment, Judy Marsh's expression showed how much she had valued those visits. "I bought a very special Dover sole for her lunch because she liked them so much."

"We have heard how your husband and you drove to the station to meet the train by which Mrs. Leithan was expected to arrive. What happened there?"

"The train was late because of the fog and when it finally arrived and she wasn't on it, we wondered if she'd missed it at Ashford and caught the next one. We waited for that as well. But she wasn't on that either."

"Have you seen her since the 18th November?"

"No."

"Have you heard from her in any way?"

"Alan, my husband, rang . . ."

"I'm sorry, but you must restrict your evidence to matters within your own knowledge." Alliter sat down.

Tarnton stood up and hitched the battered gown about his shoulders. He leaned forward slightly. "Would you not agree that Mrs. Leithan looked upon your place as a convenient boarding house, with the consequence that if she decided to change her mind about staying with you she would not feel bound to inform you of that fact?" Tarnton sat down and turned to speak to Farmen.

For a few seconds, Judy Marsh did not appreciate the full force of the insult. Then, her face reddened and her thin lips tightened. "You've no right to say that," she said shrilly. Tarnton ignored her.

Georgina Yerby was called. She told the court that her dog and Mrs. Leithan's had each gained two challenge certificates and that between herself and Mrs. Leithan there had existed an intense and bitter rivalry; so bitter on the part of Mrs. Leithan that she had resorted to bribing. Georgina Yerby gave it as her considered opinion that nothing but death would ever have stopped Evadne Leithan's attending the annual general meeting of the Cuenca Club to force the vote. Perhaps, she suggested tartly, it was no more than a just Providence that had kept her away.

Tarnton, who disliked doggy women, cross-examined her as severely as possible. He was the first to admit he gained no ground whatsoever.

The judge watched Tarnton sit down and then, when there was no re-examination, called an adjournment.

: :   : :

In the afternoon, the prosecution called a number of witnesses who had been friends of Evadne Leithan and who had frequently corresponded with her, had visited her, or had received her in their homes. Without exception, their evidence was that after the 18th November of the previous year, they had not heard from her or seen her.

The bank manager was called.

"Yes," he said, in his prim and precise voice that so exactly matched his prim and precise black coat and striped trousers, "Mrs. Leithan banked with us. She had two . . ."

"Is there any significance in the continued use of the past tense?" demanded Tarnton loudly, without bothering to stand up.

The manager looked startled.

I

"Mr. Tarnton," said the judge, "are you objecting?"

Tarnton slowly stood up. "I was wondering, my Lord, whether there is any special significance in the witness's repeated use of the past tense?"

"Is there?" the judge asked the manager.

"I . . . well . . ." The manager cleared his throat twice and straightened his already straight tie.

"The question as to whether Mrs. Leithan is alive or dead is one for the jury to decide, my Lord, not this witness."

"Quite so, Mr. Tarnton," replied the judge evenly. "And you contend that by the use of the past tense, this witness is prejudging the issue?"

Tarnton, who knew Mr. Justice Cator well enough to foresee what was to come, tried to find some way round the vulnerable position in which he had placed himself.

The judge, a man who suffered no defending counsel to dictate the course of a trial, said: "But surely, Mr. Tarnton, if the witness uses the present tense that will be––by your reasoning––equally a declaration that he believes Mrs. Leithan to be alive, which event will also be prejudging the case, will it not? May I hear what neutral alternative you suggest?"

Tarnton bowed briefly and sat down.

The bank manager continued his evidence. "She had . . . has . . ." He looked at the bench.

"Use whichever tense you prefer," said the judge, with a sweet reasonableness that was plainly aimed at counsel. "I think we shall understand."

"She had two accounts. On the 18th November, there was a credit of seven hundred and thirty-five pounds, five shillings and fourpence, in her number one account, and nine hundred pounds and sixpence in her number two account."

"Was any considerable sum withdrawn prior to that date?"

"No, sir. In the previous fortnight, the total amount was just over forty-three pounds from number one account."

"Was this sum taken out in cash?"

"There were five cheques of which only one cheque, for fifteen pounds, was in cash."

"Will you now take a period of two months prior to the 18th November. Were there any large sums of cash withdrawn?"

"There was twenty pounds on the 3rd October. The total for the two months was just under fifty pounds."

"Did Mrs. Leithan regularly draw cash?"

"If by regular, sir, you mean the same amount on the same day of each week, the answer is no. But I have checked the records and in the past year there were only three consecutive weeks in which she drew nothing and I know she was on holiday then."

"Will you tell the court how much has been withdrawn from these two accounts since the 18th November?"

"Nothing, sir."

"Not a penny?"

"No."

"Are you aware of any capital that Mrs. Leithan possessed outside of the two accounts we have been discussing?"

"From time to time, sir, she has come to me and asked my advice on investing small sums. Her share certificates and certificates of other investments, such as premium bonds and savings certificates, were lodged with the bank."

"At the request of the police, was the safe deposit box opened in which these certificates were stored and is this the list of the contents you drew up?" Alliter handed both the original and a copy to the court.

"It is," said the manager, as he accepted the single sheet of paper and quickly glanced at it.

"Can you say whether or not Mrs. Leithan had any capital other than is represented here?"

"I cannot answer that."

"Will you please give the court your considered professional opinion as to whether you believe it likely that Mrs. Leithan possessed large sums of money you know nothing about?"

There was a loud, but incomprehensible muttering from Tarnton, that drew the attention of the jury: he shrugged his shoulders and managed to look as if the vindictive behaviour of the prosecution was almost more than even he could bear.

"I think it unlikely," replied the manager.

"Do you know if any of Mrs. Leithan's capital was encashed either just before, or at any time after, the 18th November?"

"She had no access to her safe deposit box after the 5th September. Our records show that."

Alliter sat down.

Tarnton stood up. "Would you call yourself Mrs. Leithan's confidant?"

The manager pursed his lips. "No."

"She doesn't consult you on her every move?"

"Of course not."

"If she decides to invest some of her money where she wishes, she doesn't have to come to you for permission?"

"No."

"You admit she might not have always sought your advice and might have invested her money without your ever knowing anything about it?"

"Obviously, that's possible. But as I said before, I don't think it's likely since she always came and saw me first."

"You are then, determined, even against your own admissions, to proclaim your own indispensableness?"

Tarnton sat down.

Witnesses gave evidence that none of the stocks, shares, and securities, known to belong to Evadne Leithan had been cashed within two months prior to the 18th of November, or since that date.

Mallory took the stand.

"I am a partner in the firm of Enty, Mallory, and Cobalt. We have handled the affairs of the Leithan family since there was a family reconciliation." Mallory, grey-haired and with heavily-lined face, spoke pedantically. "In acting for Mr. Leithan, we have had occasion to examine the will of his father, Reginald Leithan. This will was, in many respects, an unusual one, but expert advice holds it to be legally enforceable. The provisions are complicated, but their essence is as follows: the capital is left on trust to Charles Leithan, the testator's only child, and in the event of his marriage the income is to be divided jointly between his wife and himself. On the death of either party, the money is to vest absolutely in the survivor and his or her children, and if the parties are divorced the money is to vest absolutely in the innocent party."

Alliter looked up from his brief. "Thank you, Mr. Mallory. I wonder, now, if we can run through the terms of this will again to show the jury their practical effect? Charles Leithan received all the income from the trust fund until he married?"

"That is correct."

"And once married, he and his wife shared the income equally?"

"Yes."

"There is a provision which says that if one party divorces the other, the trust fund comes to an end and the capital goes to the innocent party. Very broadly speaking, that means that should either of them commit adultery, for example, and be found out and divorced, he or she will lose all claim to the trust money?"

"Yes."

"If one party dies, the capital goes to the other party?"

"Yes."

"What is the capital at the present moment?"

"Almost two hundred and fifty thousand pounds."

There was a quick murmur of sound from the public. There was no cross-examination.

Sarah Pochard went into the witness-box. Her figure was emphasised by a very tight sweater, her face was heavily and badly made-up with the mouth a deep gash of violent red. She gave her name and address.

"I was behind the hedge and I heard 'em talking," she said.

"Heard whom?" asked Alliter.

"Him and her, of course."

"There is no 'of course' in this courtroom," said Mr. Justice Cator, in a voice straight from the Arctic.

She gulped heavily as she glanced nervously at the bench.

"Whom did you hear?" repeated Alliter.

"Mr. and Mrs. Leithan. They were rowing." She looked again at the judge. He continued to write in his note-book.

"Do you know about what?"

"It was on account of him having a bit of goods. She said as she was going to divorce him . . ."

Tarnton objected at the same moment as the judge said: "We can't have that, Mr. Alliter."

"Quite so, my Lord." Alliter addressed the witness. "You may not tell us what you heard Mrs. Leithan say."

She fiddled with the fringe of her sweater—it clashed with the colours in her skirt.

"You told us they were having a row."

"Not much they weren't."

"What part did the prisoner take in this?"

She hesitated. "I don't know what you mean."

"Was he angry? Furious?"

"Him?" She looked scornfully at Leithan. "He was tryin' to excuse himself. Said even if he had gone and seen her in the afternoon, meaning his . . ."

Alliter hastily interrupted. "Unless you know whom the prisoner saw, you must not tell us."

"He said he'd seen her, but they was only talking books. Made me laugh loud, that did. Then he said she couldn't divorce him because she hadn't no proof that him and the other was carryin' on."

"Was anything else said?"

"I can't remember nothing more."

Alliter consulted his proof and then bent over and spoke to his instructing solicitor. After that, he sat down.

Tarnton stood up. He stared at Sarah Pochard for some time and made certain that his expressive face was clearly visible to the jury. "Is eavesdropping one of your more frequently utilised accomplishments?"

"I weren't doing nothing of the sort."

"Not? Then were Mr. and Mrs. Leithan aware of your presence?"

"I . . . I don't know."

"I suggest that as you were behind the trees and as it's inconceivable that Mr. and Mrs. Leithan would have discussed anything of this nature in front of you, they were completely unaware of your presence. In fact, you know this perfectly well. So shall we give the rightful name to your occupation? Eavesdropping." Tarnton looked at the jury. He had the very useful faculty of telling them what he thought without speaking, so that nothing appeared in the records.

"I weren't. And no one can't say I was."

"How long were you behind the trees?"

"How would I know?"

"About how long?"

"It wasn't more'n five minutes."

"Five whole minutes? Plenty of time in which to leave unobtrusively, had you wanted to?"

"Well, I . . ."

As the witness remained silent, Alliter stood up. "If it will assist my learned friend in any way, the prosecution is not contending that this witness is a second *Chevalier sans peur et sans reproche*. But perhaps my learned friend would rather deal at length with the question of the morality of what he presumes to call eavesdropping, rather than with the words spoken by the prisoner?"

"Much obliged for the lecture," retorted Tarnton crossly. He had a great contempt for any vegetarian, and an even greater one for his learned "friend."

Mr. Justice Cator put down his pencil. He rubbed the lobe of his left ear. "Perhaps one might proceed?"

Tarnton appeared to search through the papers in front of him. He wondered how many of those in court realised that, no matter how hard he fought, he made no ground. "You didn't hear every single word that passed between them, did you?"

"Yes, I did."

"How d'you know that?"

"Well, I . . ." She did not finish the sentence.

"Quite so. The eavesdropper can never be certain she has heard everything—or even the major part of what's been said. Of necessity she's some distance from the speakers and her first worry is to remain hidden. If the speakers lower their voices, the eavesdropper gets left with nothing but a mumble."

"They was shouting."

"Are you really asking the court to believe that two people in their position would have a row over such a delicate matter at the tops of their voices?"

"She was shouting."

"We reduce the number to one. So she was shouting, but he was not?"

"Yes."

"The accused was speaking in a low voice?"

"I could hear what he said."

"Even when he was speaking in a very low voice to try and calm his wife?"

"I tell you, I heard everything."

"You find a certain pride in your attainments?" Tarnton paused, then spoke again. "How long were you kennel-maid at Lower Brakebourne Farm?"

"Not very long."

"A month?"

"Just a few days."

"You didn't like the position?"

"No, I didn't."

"Why not?"

"The dogs stank."

"All dogs smell if they're not properly looked after. Did Mrs. Leithan ever complain you weren't properly looking after them?"

"She was always on about 'em, and so was he. What's more, when one of 'em bit me so I bled something terrible, he didn't care."

"When was that?"

"The day I left."

"So you left this job in a state of high dudgeon, furious with your employers?" Tarnton sat down.

Alliter re-examined. "Had you decided to hand in your notice on the day on which you heard the argument between Mr. and Mrs. Leithan?"

"No."

"Thank you."

The court adjourned.

CHAPTER XIV

LEITHAN WAS ASTONISHED that the degradation of imprisonment and the concomitant austerity, had so little effect on him. He had thought it would break him since he had always known the luxury and the complete freedom of wealth, but it was the knowledge that he would probably have little to offer Pamela that worried him so terribly. True, he was not on a capital charge and his life was not threatened, but Phil had told him that if he were found guilty he would almost certainly lose any interest in the trust fund. He knew that, by now, Pamela's work was almost non-existent. She had failed to answer a number of letters, with the immediate result that she was sent no more: she had been unable to deliver the first of a series of articles and so had lost both the contract and the contact: unless she could begin another book almost at once, she would be failing her publishers. Her potential income had dropped almost to nothing.

He paced the cell, trying to silence his panicking mind and allow it to assure him that Pamela had succeeded once, so that she could again. But his was not the mind, when distressed, to accept logic. Scene followed scene. Pamela used up the little capital he could give her. She was forced to sell her house, when the market was low. Because she was so terribly worried, her books became worse and worse. . . .

He lit a cigarette. Until convicted, he could smoke as many as he wanted, so that he still knew a little freedom. Was there nothing he could do to help her? Surely there were friends who would help? Were there? Evadne had always gone for the glister rather than the gold, and she had always objected so much to his friends that in the end he had almost ceased to see them. Someone had once said that in every marriage there was one who loved and one who allowed love: there was equally one who claimed ground and one who allowed the ground to be claimed. If he had been less desirous of peace, he might now have been able to help Pamela. He castigated himself for the past, even while knowing that this was ridiculous. He had been no door-mat over whom Evadne had brushed her shoes. He had, despite all her opposition, lived his life as he wanted it.

The questions, the accusations, the appeals, whirled around in his mind until he seemed unable to think coherently.

The cell door opened. With a sense of shock, he looked at the warder.

"The law's come to see you," said the warder.

Obediently, he left the cell and walked down the iron steps which were protected underneath by a heavy steel net; justice must never be defeated by suicide. They went along a short corridor to one of the conference rooms.

Enty stood up. "'Morning, Charles."

Leithan noted the other was wearing a sober-coloured suit: was this a gesture of mourning? "'Morning, Phil."

He sat down at the table. The warder visually checked that he, Leithan, was in order and then left the room and shut the door. The lock loudly clicked shut.

Enty opened his brief-case and took out a thick bundle of papers. "Tarnton asked me to have a word with you, Charles. When the case is resumed, Abraham Smith will give evidence, and then the police. Without beating about the bush, Tarnton says their evidence is going to be difficult to shake."

"Difficult? Or bloody impossible?"

Enty searched among his papers and eventually found

what he wanted. "You spent all night on the eighteenth with Mrs. Breslow?"

"Yes." His memory recalled, with bitterness, the urgency with which he had made love and the wonderful peace he had found afterwards.

"Did you ever spend a night with her before?" Enty looked up and his rather coarse face seemed apologetic. "I know. We've asked you these questions before."

"Whenever Evadne was away for the night, I stayed with Pam," said Leithan dully. "But I always parked the car in the woods so that no one should see it and know where I was."

"And you can't suggest anyone who might help you to prove that?"

"Wouldn't it seem rather ironic to produce proof that I had been committing adultery for a long time?"

"Better to be ironic than to appear not to have committed adultery until the day Evadne vanished." Enty looked up. "Charles, something's got to shout in your favour." There was a note of desperation in his voice. "The more you sit back, the more people are going to think the worst. Tarnton asked me why you didn't seem to be fighting."

"Ask him what's the use, when the facts are openly damning me."

"That's being bloody ridiculous."

There was a short silence.

"I've a message for you, Charles, from Mrs. Breslow."

"Yes?"

"She says she's looking forward to the end of your new book, but that she didn't mean you to dive quite so deeply into the deep end."

Leithan could imagine her saying that in a tight, sharp voice.

"Let's go through the police evidence once more,

Charles. We might find something Tarnton can get his teeth into."

Wearily, Leithan dragged his mind back to the trial.

: :   : :

Abraham Smith, private detective, was a tall, upright man with a tooth-brush moustache and generous grey hair that was swept well back over his head. His clothes fitted him so well, they suggested an expensive tailor; he was able to wear a bow-tie and not look affected. He had a deep and pleasant voice in which there remained a faint suggestion of the accents of his native Devon. "I was called to the offices of Podermare and Company on the 7th September. I was instructed that on certain dates, to be given me, I was to watch Hideaway House."

"Were you given a reason for keeping watch?" asked Alliter.

"I was told that a Mr. Charles Leithan would probably visit it. My job was to gain proof of adultery."

"How were you to identify Leithan?"

"I was given a photograph of him. I also had the number of both his cars."

"Do you identify this photograph?" Alliter picked up a small studio portrait which he handed to the usher who carried it to Smith.

"This is the one."

"Is anything written on it?"

"In one corner is, 'To my beloved wife.' It is signed Charles and the date is 1951."

"Give it back to the usher, will you, please, so that my lord and the jury can see it. Exhibit No. 17, my Lord." Alliter waited to continue his examination-in-chief until the judge had examined the photograph. "Did you keep watch on the house?"

"I did."

"Do you know on what dates?"

"May I look at my notes to make certain?"

There was no objection, even from Tarnton.

Smith took a small note-book from his pocket and flicked through the pages. He found what he wanted. "September the tenth, October the first, twelfth, twentieth and thirtieth, and November the eighteenth."

"Will you tell the jury what happened on each of these dates?"

"I found a place from where I could keep observation on the house and each time I began my watch at midday. On the 10th September, Mr. Leithan arrived at . . ." He looked at his note-book. "At two o'clock in the afternoon and left at four-fifteen. On 1st October, he arrived at one fifty-one and left at seven minutes past six. On 12th October, he arrived at twelve-eleven and left at five-fifteen. On the twentieth, he arrived at four and left at six thirty-eight. On the thirtieth, I did not see him. On the . . ."

"Just one moment," broke in Alliter. "I should like the jury to be certain on one point. Did you, on the dates you've given us, keep watch after the time at which the prisoner drove away from Hideaway House?"

"In each case I stayed until two o'clock the following morning."

"Did you ever see the prisoner return?"

"I did not."

"What happened on the 18th of November?"

"I began my watch at two o'clock in the afternoon and Mr. Leithan's car arrived at forty-six minutes past three. I saw him enter the house. I kept watch throughout the night and the car remained there. I was going to knock on the front door the following morning and ask them if they would make a statement, but at seven twenty-two in the morning the right-hand curtain of one of the upstairs rooms was pulled to one side and a man looked out of the window. With the aid of a pair of binoculars, I was able to identify Mr. Charles Leithan. He appeared to be naked. Almost immediately, a lady whom I recognised as Mrs. Pamela Breslow came and leaned against him. She was wearing a nightdress. The curtain fell back into place. I left and returned home."

"You did not ask them for a statement?"

"No, sir, I decided not to."

"Why not?"

"In my opinion I had sufficient evidence to prove adultery in a court of law. Therefore, there was no need to embarrass them further. I dislike embarrassing people, sir." Smith spoke with obvious sincerity.

Alliter leaned back and rested his hands on the bench behind him. "On five separate days you watched the house and the prisoner left either just before or just after dark on four of them. On the sixth occasion, the prisoner openly stayed the whole night at Hideaway House?"

"Yes, sir."

"And the date of this was the 18th of November?"

"That is correct, sir."

"Was that the last time you kept watch?"

"No, sir. My instructing solicitors said I was to keep a further watch for a few days. The prisoner spent at least two more nights at the house."

Alliter sat down.

Tarnton turned round and questioned Farmen, then leaned forward and spoke to Enty.

"Do you wish to cross-examine?" asked Mr. Justice Cator, and only the clerk of the court, who had known him a long time, identified the slight touch of sarcasm in the other's voice. The judge was in no doubt as to why defence counsel was hesitating.

Tarnton stood upright. He gripped the sides of his gown and stared at the wall above the witness's head. "You weren't keeping a very good watch?"

"The best I could, sir," replied Smith, with deceptive humility.

"Then your best wasn't very good."

"No, sir?"

"No, it wasn't. The accused will testify that on each of the days you were watching the house and have said that he left around dark, he was . . ." Tarnton broke off as a rising murmur of voices from his left distracted his attention. Angrily, he swung round. By the first door of the courtroom, two uniformed policemen and a woman were arguing.

"What is the matter?" asked the judge sharply.

One of the policemen hastily stepped forward. "It's someone says she's got to speak, my Lord."

"*Got* to speak?"

Pamela Breslow ran forward and half tripped over a torn patch in the coir matting. She saved herself by grabbing at the back of the first row of benches in front of the dock. She stared with passionate appeal at Leithan. Then she said, so loudly she was almost shouting: "I've just seen Evadne Leithan."

CHAPTER XV

THE USHER, and then when he was ignored, the police, called for silence. It was a full minute before the hubbub of voices died away.

Mr. Justice Cator, hands clasped together in front of him, stared down at Pamela Breslow. His face was set in cruel lines. "Are you Mrs. Breslow?"

She nodded. Her face was flushed and she was breathing very hurriedly. She could not keep her hands still and was fidgeting with her skirt.

"Will you please consider your position very carefully.

In one moment, I shall ask you to enter the witness-box and take the oath. Should you thereafter be misguided enough to commit perjury—no matter how strong an emotional reason you may feel you have—criminal proceedings will be taken against you and you will suffer severe consequences."

"I've just seen her. Can't you understand that?"

"Very well." The judge turned his head slightly. "Mr. Tarnton, will you please allow the witness to stand down. You will, of course, be at liberty to recall him later on. With the knowledge that Mrs. Breslow is about to give evidence, would you then like a word with the prisoner?"

Tarnton bowed. He made his way along the line of desks and then to the dock. He spoke to Leithan as Pamela Breslow took the oath. "What the hell's going on?"

White-faced, Leithan said: "She saw her. D'you hear, she saw her."

"When did the two of you cook up this crazy scheme?"

"Crazy scheme?" Leithan stared wildly at counsel.

"Bring it to an end here and now before it does both of you too much damage."

Leithan stared at Pamela. She was looking more than her thirty-three years.

"Mr. Leithan, this is the last chance for you."

"Evadne's still alive. . . ."

Tarnton returned to his place. He saw the judge was looking at him and he shook his head.

The judge addressed Pamela. "Mrs. Breslow. You have just taken the oath. Do you realise all that that means?"

"Yes."

"What is it you wish to tell the court?"

"I was . . . I was waiting in the middle of the hall outside to be called in here. I had my back to the main

K

door. Something made me turn round suddenly and there she was. . . . You've got to do something about it, quickly. Please, you must."

"There was who?"

"Evadne Leithan."

"Are you certain?"

"Of course I am," she cried desperately. "Send someone to find her. You can't . . ."

"Be quiet," snapped the judge. "Confine yourself to answering my questions."

"But all this time . . ."

"I am usually averse, Mrs. Breslow, from committing anyone for contempt of court. Yet I have to admit that I should find less reluctance than usual in the present instance."

There was a short silence.

"What happened after you claim you saw Mrs. Leithan?"

"I shouted to her to stop. She saw who it was and ran for the door leading out to the street. I tried desperately to catch up, but she was out first and when I reached the road there were an awful lot of people around. I couldn't see her, but I tried to the left."

"I presume you were unsuccessful in your attempt to speak to her?"

"She wasn't anywhere. I rushed back here to tell you. She's laughing at Charles: she's laughing because he's being tried for her murder."

The judge unfolded his hands as he looked across at one of the two white-gloved policemen who guarded the doors into the courtroom. "Go outside, officer, and ask the constable on duty out there to come in here."

Within seconds, a young policeman entered the courtroom and stood irresolutely at the foot of the steps.

"Constable," said the judge, "has anything unusual recently taken place in the hall outside?"

The policeman cleared his throat loudly. "There was a young lady calling out, my Lord."

"Calling out what?"

"To get hold of someone called Evadne, my Lord. She was shouting and I was about to tell her to stop when she ran out on to the road. I went to see what was happening, but by the time I was outside she'd disappeared. She came back a little later on and I again went to speak to her about what was going on, like, but she evaded me and ran in here."

"You are quite certain she ran out on to the road?"

"Yes, my Lord."

"Did you see whether she was running after anyone?"

"No, my Lord."

With characteristic quickness, the judge came to a decision. "The court will adjourn, Mr. Alliter, for an hour. This will give the police a little time in which to make inquiries."

"Quite so, my Lord."

The judge stood up and the usher called for silence. He had no hope of obtaining it.

: :   : :

One hour later, the court resumed sitting.

The judge crossed the dais, walked to his chair, bowed briefly, and sat down.

An overweight uniformed superintendent gave evidence. "We've done all we could, my Lord. We've managed to contact two people who were in the hall at the time of the incident and who saw Mrs. Breslow running to the main entrance."

"Were they able to assist you?"

"Their evidence is contradictory, my Lord."

The judge's expression became grimmer. "Is that all the guidance you can offer the court?"

"Yes, my Lord." The superintendent seemed about to explain and excuse, but he rightly decided not to.

"The court will obviously have to adjourn for a longer period in order that far more extensive inquiries can be made." The judge spoke to counsel. "Mr. Alliter, for how long may we adjourn?"

Alliter successfuly covered the fact that the answer momentarily escaped him. "Surely, my Lord, that depends on how long the court wishes to adjourn for?" He blandly left it at that. Since the judge was one of the greatest living experts on criminal law and procedure, Alliter thought he could answer the question.

The judge picked out one of the text books from the small case to the right of the desk and he studied the index. He then opened the book near the beginning, read rapidly through a paragraph, and looked up.

"As is not uncommon, Mr. Alliter, the authorities are not on all fours. We are told that, once the jury have been sworn, adjournments are only allowed until the next day, but that a trial can be temporarily suspended. Again, a judge may adjourn the trial after the close of the case for the defence, but on the other hand, the court has no power to adjourn once the jury are sworn. Perhaps the best statement of the law is that an adjournment may be allowed whenever justice demands it, but that such adjournment must not be against the prisoner's interests which are, of course, that he shall not be held, before verdict, longer than is absolutely necessary. In the present case, justice most certainly demands that a fuller investigation is made into Mrs. Breslow's story and therefore this trial must be adjourned. However, I cannot conceive that it could be said no harm would be done to the prisoner's interests if this trial were to be set back to the next assize—quite apart from the practical difficulties—so that I hold it must be concluded before the end of the present assize."

"My Lord," said Alliter, "that does not allow very long for the inquiries to be made."

"I agree. But in my opinion that is something over which we have no control." The judge's cold glance rested on Pamela Breslow. "I trust the police will make fullest use of the time available."

         : :   : :

Murch's ulcer had never caused him so much distress; and as he bullied his underlings, wooed the newspapers to give him the publicity he needed, and pacified his superiors, his temper and consumption of stomach tablets rose.

In the afternoon before the trial was due to be resumed, a conference was held at H.Q.

Murch spoke first. "Our aim and object has been to prove that there can't possibly have been anyone in the hall who could have been the deceased woman."

There was some laughter at the incongruity of those words. It ceased abruptly when Murch slammed his fist down on the table. "If anyone thinks it's funny, perhaps they'll bloody well explain why?"

Fifteen uniformed men and detectives became solemn.

"If you'd all done a decent job, there wouldn't be any of this. The only witnesses you've found are two men and one constable who were in the hall—the P.C. seems to have been asleep—and one woman immediately outside on the pavement.

"Their evidence makes me want to bloody weep. The Breslow woman ran like hell, but of course she did because she's smart. But did they not see Mrs. Leithan as well? One of the men in the hall says he might have seen someone running ahead of Mrs. Breslow and this someone might have been a woman. His companion says there wasn't any second person. The woman outside swears no one came out of the building in front of Breslow. The constable didn't see a goddamn thing except what was pointed out to him."

Jaeger spoke. "Are we going to get any more evidence, sir?"

"What the hell's it look like?"

"Suppose it stays as it is now?"

"You suppose."

"It's going to be dodgy. After all, we haven't the proof to show there was no Mrs. Leithan and couldn't be. Mrs. Breslow ran out of the building and called out to the constable. When she got back to court, she was all puffed. On the facts, there could just have been someone there—someone who was Mrs. Leithan."

Murch marched up and down behind the table. "You're being real smart. Get smarter. What d'you say?"

"She's trying to pull a fast one. But, even if it's a thousand to one against, she might just be telling the truth. Suppose Evadne Leithan has been laying a false trail all this time because she loathes his guts and wants to get him into trouble over his eyebrows?"

"So you've doubts?"

"Not doubts, sir. Just the vision of a possibility. And in this case the prosecution have to prove everything to the hilt and back, and if there's any question it's not for the defence . . ."

"I know all that."

"There could easily be a question left, couldn't there?"

: :   : :

Jentry was examined by Alliter on the following morning.

"I heard a woman shout something and I looked round." Jentry, a small man with a nervous habit of suddenly shaking his head, was one of the two who had been in the hall.

"What did she shout?"

"Something like 'Stop her,' but I can't be certain of the exact words. It all took place so suddenly."

"What happened then?"

"I saw a woman run to the outside door of the hall. When she reached it, the constable began to go after her."

"Did you at any time see anyone else running in any direction?"

Jentry looked round the courtroom. His head shook and until it was realised that that was his nervous habit, it seemed as if he were emphatically denying the possibility. "I . . . I don't . . . It all happened so terribly quickly," he protested.

"The court understands that, Mr. Jentry."

"At the time, I really didn't think it all mattered."

"But with those reservations in mind, I'll put the question to you again. Did you, at any time, see anyone else running in any direction?"

"I . . . Well, I think I did." Jentry spoke with sudden pugnacity. "I think I saw someone running through the doors ahead of the second woman."

"You think this first person was a female?"

"I . . . I didn't mean it quite like that. I'm not certain."

"Would you describe him or her as tall or short, large or small?"

"I don't know."

Alliter slowly sat down. Imagination after the event, or a moment of truth?

"No questions," said Tarnton.

Krenshaw, Jentry's companion, was called.

"I heard a woman shout something so I looked round to see what was what, like. There was a woman running to the road door and I wondered what she was making such a fuss about."

"Did you notice anyone else running?"

"There wasn't anyone else. I can swear to that."

"You are swearing to it," snapped the judge.

Krenshaw appeared unabashed. "There wasn't no one else around. Except for the copper, that is."

"Would you judge that anyone could have left the hall without your seeing her between your hearing the call and looking up?"

"Not possible. It was all instantaneous, like."

"Thank you."

"No questions," said Tarnton.

P.C. Gerdhaw was called. He gave his evidence smartly, but clearly with distaste. "I was on duty in the hall, sir, and I was guarding the two doors into this courtroom. I was marching back towards the second door when I heard a cry of 'Stop her'. I turned round and saw a woman, whom I have since identified as Mrs. Pamela Breslow, running to the street doors. I went after her to see what was wrong. When I reached the door and stepped outside, I could not see her because of the large number of people around."

"Did you see anyone else running to that door?"

"No, sir." Gerdhaw wanted to be allowed to explain why it had taken him those vital few seconds before he responded to the cry—he had been hesitant about leaving his post of duty for a woman who seemed to have no reason for her call—but he was, of course, given no such chance.

There was no cross-examination.

Miss Elizabeth Casey was called. A stern-looking woman, approaching old age, her voice was surprisingly gentle. "I was walking along the road and as I neared the steps to the building I saw a young lady come running out. I have since learned she is Mrs. Pamela Breslow. She went along the road and very soon disappeared behind a number of people who seemed to belong to a party."

"Did you see anyone else leave the building?"

"I did not."

"Do you think you would have noticed if anyone had run out ahead of Mrs. Breslow?"

"I should."

"To make it perfectly clear to everyone, Miss Casey, can you be certain you were watching the exit to this building for a reasonable period of time before you saw Mrs. Breslow leave it, and watching it sufficiently closely that had anyone come out you must have seen them?"

For the first time, she hesitated. "I certainly think so," she finally said, "but I could not say I am completely certain. I might have been looking away at one time. I do remember seeing a very charming child in reins and I was surprised to see anyone so carefully dressed."

Alliter decided not to put any more questions. Her evidence, and that of the others, was almost conclusive, even allowing for Jentry. Yet what about the word "almost"? Having practised a great deal in the criminal courts, he was only too aware of the utter fallibility of human eye-witnesses: men and women would swear in all honesty to having seen something that they could not have done, and to not seeing something they must have done. So, bearing that in mind, how did the equation work out? Four witnesses, almost unanimous, against one woman who would lie herself to hell and back to save the man she loved? The answer seemed obvious. Yet he could still wonder if it was, even if that doubt was very slight. He considered the police evidence to come: the proof that Evadne Leithan had not caught the train, that the dog had been shot with Leithan's revolver, the human hairs on the brambles, the handbag, the suitcase, the nation-wide search for the missing woman. He thought of the already proven evidence. Evadne Leithan had drawn no money since the eighteenth, she had not attended a meeting it was certain she would have attended had she been alive, Leithan had avoided compromising himself with Pamela Breslow until the night of the eighteenth, after which it no longer mattered if he were compromised since the trust fund had become his and the divorce clause was no longer operative. . . .

"Thank you," said Alliter.

"No questions," said Tarnton.

"Detective-Inspector Jaeger," said Alliter.

CHAPTER XVI

THERE WERE old lags who swore that Mr. Justice Cator was the hardest judge on the bench: unwittingly, they were paying tribute to the way in which he invariably cut through all the smoke-screens laid by the defence and so arrived at the truth. Nothing so distressed an old lag as the truth.

". . . The evidence of Mrs. Pamela Breslow," said the judge in his cold, incisive voice, "will receive your immediate attention, members of the jury, and you must assess it with the very greatest possible care. For if she saw Mrs. Leithan in this building, you do not need me to tell you that there is only one possible verdict you can bring.

"It is my duty to point out to you, as Mr. Alliter has already done so, that in this connection you have to consider three questions. Did Mrs. Breslow see Mrs. Leithan in the hall? Or did she erroneously, but in good faith, think she saw Mrs. Leithan? Or did she lie about the incident in a desperate attempt to try to save the man she has admitted she loves?

"In order to answer these questions, you first have to examine the evidence of Mrs. Breslow and of the four witnesses, Mr. Jentry, Mr. Krenshaw, Miss Casey, and P.C. Gerdhaw. Mr. Jentry says he thinks he may have seen a second person running out of the building immediately after Mrs. Breslow called out, while the other three are certain they saw no one. Both Mrs. Breslow's evidence and her actions are consistent with her claim that she saw Mrs. Leithan, but, equally, they are consistent with the behaviour you would expect were she wishing to establish a lie.

"You will closely consider the testimony of these four witnesses and it may be, I do not for one moment say it will be, that you will still remain a little undecided about what to believe. You have doubts. It is now that you will examine the wider aspects of the case—facts you may very well have to consider again at a later stage of the trial and in a different context—in order to assist yourselves in coming to the necessary conclusions. You saw Mrs. Breslow in the witness-box, and I venture to suggest that there will be no objection from the defence when I say that it is perfectly obvious that she is so strongly attached to the accused that there is nothing she will not do to try to save him in his present trial: indeed, when pressed by the prosecution, she said that she had not lied when she claimed she saw Mrs. Leithan, but that she would have been perfectly prepared to do so. Here, then, is a possible motive to explain why Mrs. Breslow might lie or a reason why, in an overwrought state she might imagine she saw Mrs. Leithan.

"How are you finally to decide whether to believe or disbelieve Mrs. Breslow's story? Let me suggest that it will be by considering the further problem: is Mrs. Leithan alive or dead? This was what I meant by considering the evidence within two different contexts. You first examine it to discover whether you believe Mrs. Leithan to be dead, in which case Mrs. Breslow's evidence must be a lie, and then, if that is your opinion, you examine it again to decide whether Mrs. Leithan died at the hands of the accused.

"Members of the jury, when there is no body but a

man is charged with murder, the evidence of death has to be utterly and completely watertight. How watertight is the evidence in this present case? To find out, let us examine the life of a person, in Mrs. Leithan's position, in the world to-day. She needs food and shelter and in order to gain both she has either to be given them or she has to buy them. . . ."

            : :   : :

The jury room was dirty and it smelt because of the two lavatories that were at the far end. On the wall hung a reproduction of Landseer's "The Monarch of the Glen" and in the fireplace a coke fire struggled to stay alive. On the oblong table were paper, pencils, blotting-paper, three water containers and three plastic mugs. Around the table, nine men and three women tried to reach a decision.

"She's dead. She must be. If she isn't, why's the dog dead?"

"And why was her hair on the bramble?"

"And what's she been living on all this time? Air?"

"And why should she let the trial go on? She wasn't mental."

"And didn't the judge make it clear enough what he thinks?"

"Yes," agreed the woman, who wore strangely-shaped glasses. She was plump and her looks suggested that twenty years ago she had been reasonably good looking. She was dressed in very ordinary clothes. "But suppose . . ."

"Could *you* live on nothing for over two months? With the Government deliberately forcing the prices up? Could you?"

"And what about the dog? I suppose it shot itself?"

"Didn't that judge say no woman ever willingly let go of her handbag?"

"I . . . I was thinking," she said.

Someone doubted it.

"I was thinking that it could just have happened as that woman said: she could have seen Mrs. Leithan in the hall. I know it sounds all queer, but can't you see what I'm trying to say? I suppose you all think I'm being silly, but I couldn't live with myself if I said he did it and somewhere inside me I was thinking all the time, suppose she *was* telling the truth or suppose she *might* have been telling the truth? What I mean is, I know what it all looks like, like you keep saying to me, but there isn't a body, is there, and so she could just still be alive, couldn't she? Terrible things have happened in the past. My husband was telling me about it last night. He'd read about it in one of the Sunday papers. They hanged a man in England and the man he was supposed to have killed turned up."

"That didn't happen recently, I know."

"I think it was in sixteen hundred and . . ."

"For Gawd's sake, the world's spun on a bit since then."

"Suppose we did something like that? I mean, suppose she just had a heart attack like the barrister for the defence suggested?"

"Then she couldn't have been outside the court and the Breslow woman's lying, like we all say. And who shot the dog? And why was her hair on the bramble where she was dragged to the road? And what was a woman like her doing in the middle of a wood?"

"I don't know. But can't you see what I'm trying to say, that it could have happened? And the judge said to us we had to be absolutely certain. I couldn't live with myself if I thought that . . . Well, I'm not quite certain where I was, but . . ."

      : :   : :

THE CLERK OF THE COURT: Members of the jury, have you agreed on your verdict and do you find Charles

Protheus Leithan guilty, or not guilty, of the wilful murder of Evadne Mary Leithan?

FOREMAN OF THE JURY: Not guilty.

: :   : :

Tarnton went into the robing-room. He dropped his brief on to the table in amongst the clutter of wig boxes, blue and red bags, note-books, text books, and odd articles of clothing. He removed his wig and untied the tabs from about his neck. He sighed and caressed his forehead.

Farmen entered. "What a glorious thing must be a victory, sir. The greatest tragedy in the world, my Lord, except a defeat."

"You go and explain that to the judge," said Tarnton dryly.

"Not on your nelly. If I know anything about old Ice-Blood, he's trying to decide whether the jury should be hanged, drawn, and quartered, or really punished severely."

"A trifle energetic in showing his feelings, wasn't he, Edward?"

"Energetic? He practically jailed everyone in sight for contempt of court."

"If I ever hand out medals for courage, remind me to give the first one to the Breslow woman. She knew she was fighting impossible odds, yet she went on to win. Our Mr. Leithan's a damned lucky man."

"I usually go for blondes."

"I know. I've had the misfortune to be introduced to one of them." Tarnton took off his wing collar and fitted it into his wig box together with his wig and tabs.

"Thanks! You know something, if Mrs. Breslow were free I reckon I'd change my tastes. Not a blood pressure soarer, but she's certainly something special."

Alliter entered the room and he heard the last few words. "What peerless woman is this?"

"The incomparable Mrs. Breslow," replied Tarnton, and hoped for signs of annoyance.

Alliter smiled blandly. "Quite a girl, but rather silly."

"Silly?" asked Farmen.

"Successful violence breeds a train that travels on tracks which run out of sight."

"Too many boiled cabbages," muttered Tarnton rudely.

Alliter's junior and Enty entered the room together.

Enty spoke to Tarnton. "Leithan wants to thank you before you go."

Tarnton attached a semi-stiff collar, in which he had placed his tie, on to his back collar-stud. "How is he?"

"Surprised."

"Who isn't?" He secured the front of the collar and tied his tie, then studied his reflection in the mirror. "Still, with a girl like that around one shouldn't be surprised by anything. Ah, well, that's the way the world works. Sometimes the women are for you and sometimes they're against. I'm defending one next week who tried to separate her lover's head from his neck with a blunt axe."

"Too much red meat," said Alliter, and none of his listeners was certain whether he was joking, or not.

: :   : :

"Well," said Jaeger, "that was a ripe bastard, that was!"

"Outrageous," snapped Murch. Somewhere deep inside him there was a rumble. "God, my guts!"

"Coming on bad, sir?"

Murch stood in the middle of the hall outside the courtroom. "Your case wasn't properly prepared and the A.C.C. will go to town on it. The police have been made to look idiots."

"Aren't the courts often doing that to us, sir?"

"Only when the person in command of the çase can't bloody well be bothered to present his evidence properly."

Jaeger looked at the clock on the far wall and realised that his wife would have cooked dinner for him since he had forgotten to ring through to say he would not be back. The dinner would now be a burnt offering.

"Goddamn it, they can't honestly believe she saw the old cow," exclaimed Murch.

"Looks like they did, sir."

"Can't we charge them?"

"With being stupid?"

"There'll be a conference to-morrow at nine sharp. If it's the last thing I do, I'll find out what went wrong and why." Murch lit a cigarette. "She's a bitch."

"Yes, sir. But if I was Leithan, I'd be very proud of the fact."

: :   : :

Enty had suggested that Leithan and Pamela leave by a side exit to escape both the newspaper men and the public. By accepting his advice and the services of a friendly usher as guide, they were able to step out on to an almost deserted pavement.

It was a typically raw January night. The sky was overcast and the air was coldly moist, promising more rain very soon. The roads were still wet and the traffic sprayed the pavements with filthy water.

Leithan, for the moment oblivious of the cold, stood in the centre of the pavement. He looked upwards, and in his mind the clouds were not there and he was staring at the stars. In the cell, he had wondered if he would ever see the stars again.

He tightened his hold on her hand. "I . . ." He looked down at her. "Let's hurry and shake the dust of the town off our feet."

They began to walk. He heard a small sound from her

and in the light from a street lamp he saw that she was crying. He came to an abrupt halt.

She wiped her eyes with her free hand. "I'm being a stupid woman. But I feel as if for the past few weeks someone has been hitting me with a crow-bar and that they've only just stopped. The relief's almost more than I can bear."

"Are you asking for the man with the crow-bar to start up again?"

"Don't be a fool. Kiss me, Charles, right here."

"Pam . . . did you see her?"

"I saw her, Charles, I saw her. It doesn't matter what anyone says, I saw her. Now shut up and kiss me."

He kissed her.

They resumed walking and crossed the road to the car-park in which she had left the Rapier. She took the keys from her pocket. "Here you are, Charles."

"Shall we go home?"

"Unless you want to ignore a meal fit for a king."

"It sounds as if you didn't doubt I'd be back?"

"Of course I didn't."

He unlocked the car door and climbed in, then opened the near-side door for her. They fixed their safety-belts.

Leithan started the engine. He wondered, in an absurd way, whether it was really he who was about to drive the car back to Lower Brakebourne Farm.

"Love me?" asked Pamela.

"All there is." He went to lean across to kiss her and the safety-belt prevented his doing so.

"Let's get back home, Charles. I'm so scared that if we don't hurry I'll begin to bawl like a baby and you'd get so terribly embarrassed."

"D'you really think anything you did would embarrass me to-night?"

"Of course." She smiled. "You're such a prude."

L

He could just make out the crinkly lines about her mouth and the shine of her eyes. He unlocked the hand-brake, reversed, and drove out on to the road. "D'you know what all married servicemen are asked by their mates before they go on leave?"

"I'll buy it."

"What's the second thing you're going to do when you get home?"

"Charles, you're almost being crude! Remind me to kiss you crudely the moment we arrive. If there's anything that would do me good right now, it's crudity."

They reached the countryside and left behind them the ugly, sprawling, collection of houses and bungalows which mirrored a pattern that was cursing all England.

The headlights picked out hedges, gaunt and leafless trees, and bare fields. Even if they were on a main road, they were still surrounded by country.

He felt the slime of prison slough off him with every mile they travelled. Soon, it would be a memory that would have consciously to be recalled, but for the moment there was piquancy in the fact that he was still near enough to it to use it as a standard of comparison.

He took his left hand off the steering wheel and felt her knee. "You still haven't asked me what I'm going to do second."

She chuckled.

: :   : :

Pamela had chosen the meal as an act of faith.

The Malasol caviare had been sent down from Fortnum and Mason. Mrs. Andrews had seen the account and had looked at the caviare with shocked surprise. The Poulet à la Périgord that followed had taken many hours of patient preparation.

Leithan was pouring out the last of the Bienvenues Batard-Montrachet when Pamela said: "Mrs. Pauls was very solicitously asking me how you were."

"Grubbing for scandal. I trust you gave the old bitch an earful." They had finished a bottle of champagne as an apéritif and Leithan was finding that that, together with the wine they had had during the meal, was affecting him far more than it should have done.

"I told her you'd soon be around to answer for yourself."

Leithan lifted his glass. "To you."

They drank.

"When I see her, I'll give her something more to chew on," he said. "I'll tell her that the date of our marriage will be as soon as possible, if not sooner."

Pamela put down her glass.

"What's wrong?"

"Nothing, Charles."

"Yes, there is. I know that look from old. I learned about it the very first time I suggested we might have dinner together. What's the matter?"

"Charles . . . Charles, we can't marry."

"Who's going to stop us?"

She stared at him. "I saw her. She's still alive."

He gulped down the wine in his glass and did not consciously taste it. "What's the matter, cold feet? You've always called a spade a spade before, so come out with it now and tell me I murdered her."

"Don't be ridiculous."

"You never really saw Evadne at the trial, did you? You only saved me out of a sense of duty which you imagined you owed me and very wisely you're not going beyond that. Evadne was a bitch. I'll call a spade a spade. The biggest bitch I've known. She made my life a hell. I was rich and could afford to do what I wanted, but her mockery turned life into hell. Hell's always in the mind, you know. I was just as mentally miserable as some dirty starving beggar who loses his last sixpence. Maybe you're like the rest of the world and reckon I ought to have grinned and borne it because it wasn't really at all bad since I'd a lovely house and farm and enough money to travel or do whatever else I wanted—but those things only exist as a relief in the minds of the onlookers. I've never told you before, but she made me think of suicide. Did you know that if the barrel of a loaded shotgun is filled with water, it'll atomise a man's head. The column of water becomes like a column of steel. No time for pain, and what else prevents half the population killing itself off?"

"For God's sake stop it, Charles."

"If I had killed her, I was entitled to. Eye for eye, tooth for tooth. But our revered law daren't think that straight and apparently neither do you. Are you afraid that what happened once can happen again?"

"Charles, it's terrible to talk like this. You've had too much to drink."

"*In vino veritas.* Listen to the truth gushing from my lips. I think you're making the right and proper judgment. If you step out of my life now, you're a heroine. But if you married me, you'd be marrying a murderer and that would surely make you a fool. Lightning strikes the same place many times when there's a conductor to guide it. You couldn't live with me, knowing what I'm supposed to have done. Think of all the questions in your mind! Was it with the gun, a blunt instrument, a rope noose? They've got to give me my gun back now. Funny, isn't it?"

Pamela stood up. "I'm going, Charles."

"Where?"

"Home?"

"Getting scared?"

"I just can't stand this."

"You're not going anywhere."

"Not even you are going to stop me, Charles."

He watched her leave the room. Let the women win

the battles and the men were lost, sunk without trace. God! Could he really think in terms of winning and losing when on the table were the remains of a victory feast? A pyrrhic victory? Was that a fair description of a situation in which a man destroyed everything he wanted, everything he sought, everything he had dreamed about?

He heard the car come round from the garage and go down the drive. The sound slowly drifted into silence. He wanted to get drunk, violently, degradingly, drunk, because then he might find relief.

He went into the kitchen and down to the cellar and picked up the first bottle he could. Red, white, rosé, still or sparkling—what did it matter?

CHAPTER XVII

LEITHAN WOKE UP. He remembered the last time he had been drunk: twenty years previously, when he had been working for the Admiralty. They had refused to let him go to sea, saying he was far more valuable ashore as a man of letters. A man of letters! Twenty years could do a lot to a man's reputation.

He listened to the world. A robin was calling, the dogs were yowling, and from somewhere far away came the faint boom of a diesel tractor. Overhead, he heard the sounds of pattering feet crossing the loft boards. Evadne had waged continuous war on the mice of the house, but although she had won battles she had never gained a victory.

A pyrrhic victory. He remembered what had happened the previous night and was shocked to discover he had behaved so stupidly.

He sat up and his head began to ache. He looked at

his watch and saw it was almost nine o'clock. If the world outside had remained the world outside, Deakin would be mucking out the cows, Mrs. Andrews would have left Ashford, and Pamela . . . He stared at the second, and empty bed.

He washed and shaved, went downstairs and prepared breakfast. By the time he had finished his second cup of coffee, he felt reasonably clear-headed. He looked about him and saw an empty bottle of Château-Margaux. Perversely, that hurt as much as anything. That he could have used so great a wine solely in order to get drunk.

There was a knock on the front door. He looked through the kitchen window and saw a girl he did not recognise walking up to talk to Jaeger, who was waiting by the door.

What in the hell was Jaeger doing there? It was all over and done with, bottled up and thrown away.

He went along the passage, through the sitting-room, and into the hall. He opened the front door and before he could say anything, the girl called out: "Good morning, Mr. Leithan, I'm Molly Quayle. Mrs. Breslow took me on as kennel-maid. I do like the Cuencas, they're such darlings."

Leithan stared at her. Jolly hockey-sticks. "I'll have a word with you later." His anger increased when he realised she was regarding him with an obvious determination to record everything about him: writing home to jolly-d mother to say what a murderer looked and spoke like? "Come in," he said to Jaeger.

Jaeger stepped into the hall and Leithan shut the door on the fascinated girl.

The detective walked across and stood in front of the collection of guns. "I was in London the other day and I saw a Cantriner En Wien repeating air-rifle going for two hundred pounds. I wouldn't have called it as good an example as yours."

Leithan looked up at the short barrelled, leather covered, butted rifle, which was inlaid with a profusion of gold and silver.

"There was an early flintlock pistol in the same shop," continued Jaeger. "It was badly damaged—the top half of the flintlock was missing and the trigger was broken. I thought I might buy it for something under a couple of quid. The polished and perfumed assistant very loftily told me that it cost thirty guineas."

"Have you come here to talk antique guns?"

"I'll admit I'd like to, sir, but I don't suppose you'd want to waste your time that way."

"You're supposing right."

"No hard feelings, I hope?"

"How should I know what you'd call them? After all, you did your damnedest to have me convicted of murder."

"No, sir, not like that. I've a job to do and I like to do everything as well as possible. There's nothing personal in it."

"Nothing personal when you spent night after night out in my fields searching for her body and making certain you woke me up so that I knew all about it?"

"Call it a strong sense of duty, sir."

"I'd call it lots of things."

"I bet." The good humour of the D.I. became even more apparent.

Against his will, Leithan found his anger disappearing.

He had never welcomed the need to be rude and when faced with good humour he could only respond to it. "Let's go in there," he said finally. He pointed to the sitting-room.

Mrs. Andrews entered the house through the front doorway. She smiled delightedly. "Good morning, Mr.

Leithan, sorry to use this door, but the other's still locked. Cold wind, isn't it? As I said to Norah—she's the one whose young brother ran off with Betty and he refused to marry her even though a kid's coming despite her mother saying it isn't—much more of this cold and we'll all have to buy more of that slate what the Coal Board sells as coal. How about some coffee?"

"Thanks."

Leithan closed the door of the sitting-room behind himself. "That's the first time she's seen me since I went to prison. I've been tried for the murder of my wife and found not guilty. Yet all she's interested in are the scandalous doings of the neighbours."

"Far more important to her. In any case, I'll guarantee she was certain you couldn't possibly be guilty."

Leithan picked up the silver cigarette-box and offered it to the other. "Do you? I forget."

"I usually only handle a pipe, sir."

"Of course. Light up if you want to."

Jaeger took his pipe from his pocket and filled the bowl. As he finished tamping down the tobacco, he looked up. "There's nothing official about my visit. It's completely off my own bat."

Leithan hoped the coffee would not be long. His headache had returned with added intensity.

"I've been wondering, sir, if you'd set a tidy mind to peace?"

"I don't follow you."

"You must know that if you tell me the full story now it couldn't harm you at all?"

"Are you still accusing me of murdering her?"

"I'm just wondering about the facts, sir. Like I said, I've a tidy mind."

"Take it with you out of this house. What are you after? Trying to get your own back any way you can? If I did kill my wife, it's pretty obvious Mrs. Breslow was lying. I suppose you'd give anything to land her for perjury and send her to jail?"

Jaeger lit his pipe. He stared with appreciation at the ingle-nook fireplace which had on the right-hand side the original bread oven. "I've one feeling for Mrs. Breslow, sir. Respectful, but very strong, admiration."

"D'you expect me to believe that when you admit you think she lied?"

"In her case, sir, the greater the lie, the greater the respect. Look, I'm not here to try to cause any sort of trouble. Back at the station, they don't even know I'm here and there won't be a single record of what goes on. Maybe you say it's a hell of an impertinence on my part; to that I say I've done twenty years, or more, in the force and if I've learned anything, it's how to be impertinent but not blush. I've a strange mind, Mr. Leithan, and that's the God's truth, and I never know whether to be proud or ashamed of it. It worries like hell over things that don't fit, and there's nothing I can do about it. I saw a new office building in London and the water tanks weren't exactly in the middle of the top: it worried me for days and days. Take your trial. What's the outcome? Untidiness. Is Mrs. Leithan alive or dead? If she's dead, who killed her? If she's alive, why was the dog killed? Can't you see, I must know the answers for myself. The police have failed, but between you and me they're pretty philosophical about such things. But in me, there's an ache of untidiness. Did Mrs. Breslow see your wife in the courthouse? If Mrs. Breslow didn't see her, is she dead? Did you kill her?"

Leithan drew on the cigarette and mentally savoured the irony of a detective-inspector who approached the discharged murder suspect and begged for the truth. He scraped ash into the ceramic ash-tray by his side. "If I knew the answers, I wouldn't pass them on."

The D.I. did not try to hide his disappointment.

"It would be too easy a way of releasing a conscience. I've always thought that expiation of a sin should never be allowed to be by confession, because that gives relief too easily and so cheapens the sin. But I'll tell you that we had seven dogs. Six of 'em I could have throttled with my bare hands. The seventh liked me more than anyone else in the world and there was only one living creature in this world I loved more."

"Was the seventh dog the one that died?"

"Stymie."

"You didn't shoot her?"

Leithan shook his head.

CHAPTER XVIII

JAEGER PARKED his car in front of Hideaway House. He climbed out and went across to the front door. As he knocked, he shivered. The wind had knives to its edges.

Pamela Breslow opened the door. Jaeger was shocked by the signs of strain on her face: she was looking far more worried, even, than at the trial. He wondered why she was not at Lower Brakebourne Farm. "Could I have a few words with you, Mrs. Breslow?"

"Come in," she answered dully. "The place is in a frightful mess, but I don't expect you'll worry."

He followed her into the sitting-room in the roundel. She had not exaggerated. The room looked as though it had not been tidied or cleaned in weeks.

"Care for a drink?" she asked.

"I'm afraid it's a bit early for me."

"It isn't for me. Change your mind?"

"Could I have a beer, then?"

"Guinness or light ale?"

"A light ale, please." It was pretty obvious there had been some sort of bust-up between them. He watched her cross the room and pour out a strong whisky for herself. He hated his job when he saw what it could do to people.

"I suppose you've come to arrest me?" she demanded. She took a pewter mug from the corner cupboard, a bottle, and an opener. She returned and handed them to him and stared at him with a challenging hate in which was an appeal.

"No."

"Why not? You think I committed perjury."

"Does it matter what I think?"

"Doesn't it?"

He smiled. He put the mug down on the floor to the right of four stacked volumes of the *Encyclopædia Britannica*, opened the bottle of beer, and poured it out. When he straightened up there was a twinge of pain from his back to remind him that old age was shouting from the sidelines. "Your health."

She lifted her glass slightly, returned to the second arm-chair. "The judge practically ordered the police to throw me into jail."

"Mr. Justice Cator is a man of decided opinions. But as far as the police are concerned, we can't do anything until we know the truth. When we can be certain whether Mrs. Leithan is alive or dead, then we can know whether you committed perjury." He hesitated, then said very quickly: "As far as I'm concerned, if it was perjury it was a wonderful perjury."

She drank quickly, looked at him and then away, picked up a letter which had been lying on the arm of the chair and fiddled with it. It was one of the letters she had received informing her that her work was no longer wanted.

"How d'you like those dogs of Mr. Leithan's?" he asked.

"Dogs?"

"I'm afraid I can never remember the name of the breed."

Impatiently, she forced herself to concentrate. Unless she wanted to be a fool, she must realise that no matter what he had said, this visit was probably a hostile one. "Cuencas." She drank some of the whisky. "There are a hell of a lot of breeds I prefer."

"Mr. Leithan was saying he'd like to get rid of the remaining six."

"Wouldn't you? She only kept them because they offered her a chance to come out on top. She wasn't a doggy woman: just someone who used dogs to give herself something she'd never otherwise have found. If the breed had been established in the country ten years before it was, she'd never have bothered with it."

"Mr. Leithan must have got fed up with them?"

"Ask him about the joys of cutting up paunch!" She finished the whisky and stared down at the glass.

"I suppose he hated the lot of them?"

"Not Stymie. Charles is one of those people who, underneath a rather calculated exterior, longs for, and needs, affection. Stymie gave that to him in bucketfuls. They were practically inseparable—and did that annoy the old bitch. Stymie wouldn't have anything to do with her." Pamela looked up. "I suppose you think it's nonsense to say Charles needs affection?"

"No, Mrs. Breslow."

"I doubt whether you really understand. Most married people get enough to see them through, even if their passion will never set the Thames on fire."

There was a short silence. "I hope everything works out all right for you," he said finally.

"What exactly do you mean by that?"

"No more than it sounds like."

"Then it's a strange thing for you to say."

"Can't a policeman wish someone good luck?"

"I don't know. I've come not to know anything." She stood up. "Have another beer?"

"Not for me, thanks. I've too much work to do." He finished his drink and then stood up. "If I don't do some of it soon, I'll be directly responsible for bursting my superior's ulcer."

He walked to the door and she followed him. As she stood in the small hall and watched him leave the house, she tried to remember all that had been said because she was desperate to know what he had wanted from her.

: :   : :

The rain came tearing across the countryside, blown at a sharp angle by the wind. It lay everywhere because the land had become too waterlogged to soak up any more moisture. The Rover shuddered to the wind, especially when clearing cover and coming parallel with a hedgeless field. The wipers were unable to keep the screen clear and for brief moments parts of it became almost opaque. Leithan slowed down, telling himself that to do so was in the interests of safety. Yet, somewhere inside him, he knew that he desperately wanted to see and speak to Pamela but was afraid of the moment of meeting, so that he wished to put it off for as long as possible. Had too much been said between them: had they passed the point of no return? They had needed all the calm they could find, yet he had, with irrational stupidity, raised a storm.

As soon as he decided he was slowing down because he was afraid of the meeting, he increased speed. Let the psychologists work that one out, he thought savagely. He turned a sharp corner and the parcel on the seat rolled over against his thigh, then rolled back. Pamela had a passion for cashmere twin-sets which she wore when she went "posh." He had bought the most expensive to be found in Ashford and although it was not one of her favourite colours, he hoped it would do as a peace offering.

Hideaway House came into sight. Water was rolling down the cowl and the very steep roof of the roundel and was overflowing out of the guttering. He noticed that two tiles were missing. Behind the house, the bare and naked trees shivered to the wind: a tall and wildgrown yew tree, seemingly incongruous in its greenery, whipped backwards and forwards.

He brought the car to a halt and then ran across to the front door which opened as he arrived at it. He suddenly remembered the twin-set and, despite Pamela's attempts to prevent his returning, he went back to the car for it.

The moment they were in the sitting-room, he kissed her and it was with a sense of utter relief that he realised she was returning his kiss with all her natural passion. "God, I've been terrified," he murmured.

She clasped her hands together behind his neck. "Of what?"

"After last night . . ."

"Let's forget there was a last night."

"Can you?"

"I did so before you came."

He kissed her again, then gave her the present. She unwrapped it, exclaimed delightedly over it, and insisted on putting it on. They both knew the colouring did not suit her, but neither cared.

"I've nothing for lunch, Charles, except cold bangers and you always turn your nose up at such plebeian fare."

"Not this time. Cold bangers and mash. Wasn't there a song about them?"

"I expect so."

"What about wine?"

"There's a choice between Algerian or Spanish red. Add some soda and imagine it's pink champagne."

He knew he had never before experienced such pure happiness. There was a wonderful joy in regaining something precious one thought one had lost. "I got tight last night," he suddenly said. "Really stinking tight."

"So the man's human!"

"So human, that all day I've had a very human headache. Not helped, either, by the fact that Jaeger turned up."

She ceased to smile. "He . . . he hasn't long been gone from here."

"What the devil did he come here for?"

"I just don't know. He paid me a heavy compliment, didn't think there was much chance of a charge of perjury, asked about all your dogs, and then left."

"There must have been more to it than that. What did he say about perjury?"

"Only that no one could do anything until the body of Evadne was found or she was discovered alive."

"Why won't he leave us alone?" Leithan began to pace the floor. "Why did you do it, Pam?"

"Do what?"

"Lie about seeing Evadne?"

"Who says I lied?"

"Of course you did."

"Please, Charles, let's forget it."

Some insanity forced him on, even when he knew it was sheer stupidity to continue. "You didn't see her. Everyone knows you didn't. D'you think I can't appreciate all the questions in your mind every time you look at me? D'you think I don't know you daren't use the true words?"

She made a sound that was close to a moan. "Charles, you must pull yourself together."

"Must I? What d'you think it's like for me with all those unasked questions around?"

"Can't you understand?" she said desperately. "There aren't any questions or accusations. You're reading into me something that doesn't exist."

They both knew it was no good.

: :   : :

Jaeger gave his name to the girl in the office of Podermare and Company. She said she would see if Mr. Stainer could spare a few minutes. As she left, Jaeger thought that if skirts became any shorter, there'd need to be a league for the protection and preservation of men. He looked out of the window and stared at the traffic in the wide main street of Tenterden.

"Mr. Stainer's free," said the girl, as she returned. "Through the passage there, and first door on the right."

Jaeger went through to the indicated room.

"Good afternoon, Inspector," said Stainer. He was almost a refugee from Edwardian times. He had a neatly cut imperial beard that was grey, he used a monocle, wore a solid albert that looped across his very ample stomach, and he obviously enjoyed as many of the pleasures of life as he could.

Jaeger sat down in the worn leather arm-chair and asked for, and was granted, permission to smoke his pipe. "Remember Mrs. Leithan, sir?"

"There's hardly been enough time to forget her."

"She asked you to engage the private detective, Smith?"

"She did. And I might add that I had no idea she usually instructed solicitors in Ashford, else I should have tried to persuade her to return to them—not that she would have done, of course—but I would not wish it to appear that I had stolen a client." He spoke with sufficient dignity to remove any trace of pomposity.

"What did you think of her?"

"My dear Inspector, do you really expect me to answer that in all honesty?" Stainer smiled and the expression made him look rather puckish. "If I were to admit to my private feelings regarding some of my clients, I should have a very heavy crop of slander suits on my hands."

Jaeger discovered his pipe had gone out and he lit a match. "Proper bitch, wasn't she?"

"I imagine one could allude to her in such terms."

"Did she want anything other than you putting a tail on her husband?"

"I have answered all these questions before, you know."

"Yes, sir, but not to me."

Stainer sighed and pulled open a drawer from which he brought out a very ornate china snuff-box. He inhaled snuff into each nostril. "I never catch a cold, Inspector, and that is due solely to snuff. Now. What did Mrs. Leithan speak to me about? Before I answer you, have you realised that according to the verdict of the trial she may still be alive? If so, then I may be said to be her solicitor still, and between her and me there lies the privilege that always rests between solicitor and client."

"Are you claiming it, sir?"

Stainer replaced the snuff-box in the drawer. He wedged his thumbs in the pocket of his waistcoat and leaned back in his chair. "Yes, I am. In the circumstances, I feel it my duty to do so."

Jaeger smiled. "You lawyers!"

"It's the principle that counts, Inspector."

"The privilege isn't absolute, is it?"

Stainer's expression became guarded. "Isn't it?"

"You'll know far more about it than I do, but aren't I right in thinking that a privilege doesn't exist in court if the solicitor were asked to advise on criminal or unlawful proceedings?"

M

"Are you suggesting I advised Mrs. Leithan on such matters?"

"I think she came to you with the object of effecting a public mischief and needed your advice to see if she could carry it out."

"She asked for no such advice."

"Did she not want to know the various ways in which she could gain a divorce?"

Stainer looked bewildered.

"Didn't she demand to know what courses were open to her?"

"Will you assure me, Inspector, that to the best of your belief, Mrs. Leithan was contemplating a public mischief?"

"Yes, sir."

"Very well. Mrs. Leithan came to me regarding the possibility of a divorce. Right from the beginning I had to point out to her that in this country a divorce is still the consequence of certain acts, and not vice versa. The fact that evidence could not be arranged seemed to annoy her excessively, so much so that she threatened to leave this office and consult someone else. When I informed her that she was at perfect liberty to do so, she changed her mind. We discussed the various grounds for a dissolution of marriage and it became clear that if she did have one such ground, it was adultery. Further inquiry, however, demonstrated that her husband had been far too clever to give her the proof she needed. Because of this, she demanded the services of a private detective. I asked her whether the detective was to keep watch all the time. She first said yes, then no. She consulted her diary and gave me the dates on which the man was to keep watch."

"Did she give you all the dates then and there?"

"All but the last one which was, of course, the 18th of November. Frankly, she was a nuisance because after each date passed she telephoned me to discover what proof had been obtained. When I repeatedly had to reply none, she became more and more abusive, demanding to know why I wasn't doing my job. I had to inform her of what my job comprised. Finally, she gave me the 18th of November."

"When did she do this?"

"Perhaps a couple of days before."

"And that's the full history?"

"Apart from payment, that was all the contact I had with her. The last settlement I had was at the beginning of November, so that the final few accounts of Mr. Smith have not yet been met." Stainer rested his elbows on the desk and joined the tips of his fingers together to form a triangle. "You can hardly be thinking of charging the husband again?"

"No."

"Then may I inquire what you do intend to do?"

"Perhaps it's my turn to claim privilege—and this time it's absolute," said Jaeger with a smile.

: :   : :

Jaeger drove through Ashford and on to the Canterbury road. The houses began to thin out and soon he was in the countryside that to him, a townsman by choice, looked bleak to the point of ugliness.

As he approached the Braychurch turning and Roman Woods, he wondered what Yelt, the keeper, would say: probably curse with all the freedom and eloquence of a Kentish yeoman who was certain he was in the right.

Jaeger came to the turning and went down it. He drove through the village—one store and one pub—and stopped outside the keeper's cottage. Mrs. Yelt said her husband was somewhere out on the estate, trying to track down whoever had fired a couple of shots an hour or so before. Jaeger thanked her and left a message.

He went back to the A28 and parked his car on the

grass verge where Frog Wood came down to the road. He put on wellingtons and after a quick look at the sky carried a rolled-up plastic mackintosh under his arm. He pushed his way into the woods.

They were dark and dismal, and they depressed him as woods always did. He was startled by a rustling noise and when he turned sharply he saw a grey squirrel run, with undulating movement and raised tail, to a large oak tree behind which it disappeared. He was not of a sensitive nature, but it did seem to him that the echoes of death were still around.

He turned right and came to the small pond and the ride where the dog's head had been found. He continued to the spot where the small grave had been dug and the bullet, dog's body, handbag, chemist's bottle, revolver and suitcase had been recovered. On the opposite side was the patch of brambles in which the hairs had been, between the grave and the road. Suppose they had all been wrong? Signposts pointed in two ways.

He returned to the ride and looked down it. It twisted round in a semicircle, so that from where he stood he could not see, to the north, the point at which it came out to the road. He turned and went southwards. The ride reached the narrowest part of the wood and then, as he entered Roman Woods, it continued parallel to the stream.

The clay on his wellingtons grew heavier and heavier and he had to keep kicking great clods of it clear. The land on the right began to fall away to form a valley, the banks of which were thick with rhododendrons.

He came to the first of the lakes, the smallest of the three. Several birds rose from the surface, with a loud slapping of wings on the water, and he identified them as some kind of duck.

He studied the lake. Rhododendrons came down to the water and the edges were thick with reeds. The other

two lakes were much the same, but larger, yet he decided
to go forward to see them. Light rain began to fall and
he hurriedly put on the plastic mackintosh.

      : :   : :

On his arrival at the police station the following day,
Murch went straight to Jaeger's room. "What's the use
of searching the lakes again?" he snapped, as he strode
through the doorway. He reached Jaeger's desk and
leaned on it. "We dragged 'em before. In any case, the
bloody man's been found not guilty."

"I want to find the body, sir," replied Jaeger.

"All very efficient. But wasn't it you who assured
everyone the body wasn't in the woods? Wasn't it?"

"In a way, sir."

"And now you're changing your tune when it doesn't
matter?"

"I think it does, sir. Tidies things up."

"You can talk about tidy?"

"As things were, sir, we were right until we believed
that because the facts were fitting our theories so neatly,
our theories had to be facts: that because the hair on the
bramble was between the dead dog and the road, the
body must have been dragged to the road. We forgot to
discover what Leithan thought of Stymie."

"Who the hell's that?"

"The dead dog."

"Are you trying to tell me . . ."

"If he was so fond of it that he could never have shot
it, who did? If Mrs. Leithan's body wasn't dragged to the
road where did it go?"

Murch spoke loudly. "The woods have all been gone
through. There's nothing there."

"Don't forget, sir, the dog was found pretty soon after
we began in Frog Wood. But we still searched the rest
of Frog Wood thoroughly, if dutifully because by now
we thought we were wasting our time. Then we were

told we had to check all two hundred acres of Roman Woods. Now, we *knew* we were wasting our time. When you know you won't find anything, it doesn't surprise you in the least when you don't, but we even had the lakes dragged in order to stop the defence being able to get clever at the trial—of course, if you're seriously expecting to find a body in a lake, you don't admit a blank if dragging gives you no results. You move on to more efficient methods."

"Like an army of frog-men?"

"The ride runs above each of the lakes and the banks are steep, and in some places they're also relatively clear. A body would roll down into the water with some force —enough to get trapped so securely by the reeds that even if the drag came up to it, it would only pass over it."

"The keeper . . ."

"I questioned him. He reckons he's tramped most of the woods since November, but all he's done at the lakes is to feed the duck."

"You know what you're saying, don't you?"

"In what respect, sir?"

"You're saying the police made one bloody big mistake."

"Perhaps. But it wouldn't be the first time, and it won't be the last."

"D'you know what the A.C.C. is going to say if you've wasted the time of the frog-men?"

"I can guess, sir."

Murch muttered something, then turned and walked out of the room. Jaeger absentmindedly began to pack the bowl of his pipe with tobacco. He looked down at the paper-work on his desk and sighed. The telephone rang.

"Watters, sir. She was there, hooked up so well the bloke said it was as if she'd been knitted into the reeds. Three feet below the surface of the biggest lake."

CHAPTER XIX

GEORGINA YERBY was patently suspicious and resentful as she climbed out of the battered Austin Seven van and stared briefly at Lower Brakebourne Farm, which was looking beautiful and mellow against the stormy sky. She was dressed in her working tweeds: skirt and coat hung loosely against her angular figure. "I got your letter," she said to Leithan, as he closed the van door after she had climbed out.

He resisted the desire to point out that that was explicit in her presence. "I hope you'll accept them."

She put on an old and dirty mackintosh and it was difficult to know whether it was by accident or design that she ignored his proffered help. "You didn't mention a price?"

"I don't want any money for them, Georgina."

She tried not to show how relieved she was. "It's . . . It's very decent of you."

"I hope you'll have plenty of success with them."

"They're good foundation stock. I'll cross the dog with my bitch on her next heat and the bitch puppies can be put to the secretary's dog."

"Let's collect them and then have a drink."

"Not for me, thanks. I've got to get back to organise everything."

They walked round behind the belt of ornamental trees. The kennel-maid had already boxed up Nemean and Lernaean and at a word from Leithan she left to take them to the van. "I'll send you all their papers and things," he said. "We mustn't forget to notify the Kennel Club of the transfer."

"No."

They became silent. Each searched for something to say and failed. The kennel-maid returned and tried to persuade Ceryneian into the wire-fronted box. The bitch yowled and, with unusual dexterity, evaded capture until Leithan gave a hand. Erymanthian gave up without a struggle and seemed on the point of physical collapse.

"Won't you miss them?" asked Georgina Yerby.

"Not in the least."

"I'm very grateful."

That conversation ceased. Leithan longed for the peace of her departure, and she wanted to escape from the sense of obligation.

The kennel-maid collected Hippolyte and Cerberus, and Georgina Yerby and Leithan followed her to the van. A car came up the drive and, with a sense of anger, Leithan realised it was Jaeger's.

The noise from within the van became greater. The Cuencas had taken fright and were screaming for help and protection.

"I'll be off," said Georgina Yerby. She had been wondering whether she ought to say something about Evadne, but her uncertainty was now at an end because it was time to go.

"I hope you'll make up a champion at Crufts."

"It would be rather fun." She made a very great effort and said: "Pity Stymie won't be there. Well, good-bye, Charles. I'll let you know how they get on." She climbed into the van and he slammed the door shut. The engine fired at the third pull of the starter. She drove off and the noise of the dogs died away.

Jaeger left his car. "'Morning, Mr. Leithan. Is that the end of the dogs?"

"Yes."

"Can we go inside, sir? I've some news for you."

"What kind of news?"

Jaeger took the initiative and walked round to the front door. They went into the house and from the sitting-room came the shrill hum of a vacuum cleaner. "We'd better use the study," said Leithan.

When they were in the study, Jaeger said: "I'm sorry to tell you, sir, we've found the body of your wife."

Leithan's mind tried to panic, but he forced himself to think coherently. He knew he was being closely watched, but could do nothing to stop his hands trembling. "Where was she?"

"In the third lake in Roman Woods."

Leithan sat down and fumbled in his coat pocket for his cigarette-case. He remembered how Pamela had told him he would only be able to fulfil his promise as a writer if he paddled in the dung of life. Was this sufficiently dungy?

"We had to conduct a post-mortem, of course."

"Yes," said Leithan. His fingers dug into the palms of his hands.

"Mrs. Leithan died from a coronary thrombosis."

"A . . . a what?"

"Coronary thrombosis, sir, following an acute attack of *angina*."

Leithan said hoarsely: "I must have a drink." He went into the sitting-room, where Mrs. Andrews was startled by his expression, and he returned with a bottle of whisky, a soda siphon, and two glasses on a tray. He poured out two drinks without bothering to ask if the other wanted one.

"I'm afraid the story isn't a pleasant one," said Jaeger.

Leithan drank quickly. Suddenly, he remembered to hand the second glass across.

"Much of it, anyway, must be guesswork. Your wife hated Mrs. Breslow and obviously tried every possible

way to break up the relationship. When she failed, she
determined to make you suffer for it and the most obvious
way to do that was to divorce you and so cut you out of
the trust fund. Without money, she was certain you would
be lost.

"She went to the solicitors in Tenterden to discover
how to gain a divorce and learned she would have to
prove adultery. Her first way to try to do this was to
have you watched by a private detective when she was
not at home. However, you'd been too cautious and
his reports didn't provide the evidence she needed.

"When it seemed it was going to be denied her, that
divorce became more important to her than anything
else in the world: even more important than making her
Cuenca the first champion in England.

"She was certain that if she disappeared you would
become careless about your relationship with Mrs.
Breslow: further, if her disappearance looked like death,
your carelessness would be such that you would afford
her the evidence of adultery she so desperately needed.
So she decided to vanish on the way to a meeting everyone
would swear blind she'd attend while an ounce of breath
remained in her body.

"She made you drive her to the station on the
eighteenth, but wouldn't let you see her on to the platform. After you'd gone, she put her plan into operation
—and how she must have blessed the fog!

"This is where we come to the guesswork. Mrs. Leithan
was making for Margate or Ramsgate, where even in
November there would be enough people to render her
anonymous. Anonymous, that was, if she didn't have
the dog with her, because that was sufficiently unusual
to identify her immediately. She must have drugged it
before she left home with some fit and hysteria pills or
something like that, and when you'd dropped her at the

station the dog was sufficiently dopey to be put into the
suitcase without causing trouble. We know the case was
only a quarter full of clothes so that there was plenty of
room and also that there were a number of dog hairs on
the pyjamas. I suppose I'd better admit that I merely
thought that proved she took the dog to bed with her.

"She walked into the town and caught a Canterbury
bus. She left this at Frog Wood and went into the wood
along the main ride. Soon, she turned off to find a spot
in which to kill the dog.

"At first, it may seem strange she did kill it, but I'm
sure it isn't if you stop to realise that that animal had
come to mean to her far more than just a dog. It was
hers, but it gave all its affections to you and that
infuriated her: you had stolen it, just as you had stolen
the marriage. She knew, therefore, that if she killed it,
she would be destroying something you loved and that
would give her a revenge she so desperately desired. To
date, all the victories had been yours: now, you could
be made to suffer a defeat that would hurt. Finally,
when the dog was dead, she could no longer own the
first Cuenca Champion and, in her mind, it would have
been you and no one else who deprived her of this
chance. She could hate you for ever for denying her her
ambition.

"She had brought along your revolver and some
ammunition. She dug a shallow grave, rested the doped
dog by this grave, took aim, and fired. Her first shot
missed, because her mental state bordered on temporary
madness and in any case she knew nothing about revolvers.
She went much closer and fired again and this time was
successful.

"She must have been a sad and ghastly sight, revolver
in one hand, the dog a bloody mess at her feet. Everything
she had fought for had now been destroyed. Her passion

became so great that she suffered an acute attack of *angina*. The pain gripped her and all her thoughts were now turned to the relief that she must gain from her tablets. She collapsed to the ground and had to crawl across to where she'd left the handbag. In this struggle, she went through a patch of bramble and her hair was caught up on the thorns and some of it was torn out of her scalp. Eventually, she got the bottle from her handbag and she either took a tablet and replaced the screw top or else she did not even have the strength to open the bottle.

"The worst of the pain passed. Mentally confused, terribly frightened by what had almost been a fatal attack, she slowly struggled to her feet. Gone was all thought of what she had intended to do: in her mind there was only room for her need of medical attention. She stumbled back to the ride and turned on to it—and in her terrible confusion went the wrong way. She entered Roman Woods.

"She met no road, no passers-by, no one to help her—only more and more wood. Perhaps she believed her mind was playing her false and she panicked, tried to move more quickly. She came to the third lake and began to climb the ride, which is quite steep, when nature cried enough. She suffered a coronary thrombosis, died instantly, fell sideways, and rolled down the bank into the water where she was caught up in the long reeds." Jaeger finished his drink. He watched Leithan pour himself a second one.

Leithan used a handkerchief to mop his face. "Are you sure?" he muttered.

"She did not die from *angina*."

"But . . . but you said she might not have managed to unscrew the cap of the bottle which had her pills in it."

"One of the popular medical misconceptions is that if

an *angina* patient fails to take a tablet right away, he'll fall down dead. It can happen, but it's not likely."

Leithan stubbed out his cigarette and immediately lit another. He finished his drink.

"The fact that Mrs. Leithan didn't draw a large sum of money just before she disappeared is obviously because she expected to stay in a hotel. At the end of her stay, she would pay by cheque because as soon as you'd become careless enough to provide the evidence of adultery, she was returning to life."

Leithan twisted his empty glass round in his hands. He looked up. "Will Mrs. Breslow be charged with perjury?"

"I'd like to meet the jury who'd convict a woman of perjury when it was her lies that saved an innocent man from being wrongly convicted of murder."

"Thank God," whispered Leithan softly.

Jaeger stood up. "I must be off."

"Have another drink? Stay to lunch?" Leithan spoke so excitedly that the words jumbled into each other.

"I'd like to, but I can't right now."

"Some other time, then?"

"It's a date, sir." Jaeger took two paces towards the door, then he stopped. "All the personal things belonging to Mrs. Leithan that the police have been holding are outside in my car. Would you like them?"

"I . . . I think so, please." Leithan followed the other out of the house and stood by the car as the detective reached inside and brought out the revolver, handbag, suitcase, and leather collar. "I hope these won't hold too painful memories." As Jaeger spoke, he was looking at the dog collar. "By the way, Mr. Leithan, I'd throw that bottle of tablets away, if I were you—it's never safe to keep old medicine about the place."

After Jaeger had driven away, Leithan turned and stared at the house. It, the hundred and eight acres, the

cows, all were his. He walked across and felt the rough-
ness of the old bricks.

He returned to the study and poured himself out a
third whisky. How could he celebrate? The answer came
to him immediately. Continue with the ordinary routine
of life because that was the greatest gift to a man who
had so nearly lost it.

He placed the revolver, dog collar, handbag, and
suitcase, on the desk. He was glad Stymie had died
quickly.

He opened the handbag. He smelled the scent she
had always used and just for a moment he hesitated.
Then he reached inside and brought out the chemist's
bottle. Quickly, he undid the screw cap and rolled the
tablets on to the blotting-paper.

: :   : :

At first he could not see it. Then he picked it out.
The tablet that was slightly different in colour and
shape.

: :   : :

What did a man do when he was forced to choose
between two courses and dared take neither?

From the beginning, it had been obvious that Evadne's
death was the only solution. His mind, trained to
construct a whole story from a single idea, had whirled
into a series of fantasies. Shooting, stabbing, hanging,
poisoning. . . .

He had always understood his own character and had
therefore known he would never dare to poison her—but
what about the tablets she took to counter an attack of
angina? Suppose one of those was not what it should
have been? A negative would kill and because it was
negative there could be no possibility of a positive
suspicion.

He had taken one of the tablets and had tried to find

THE BENEFITS OF DEATH

some other substance that resembled it sufficiently closely
to pass for it. There had been nothing: the fawny shade
of grey appeared to be unique. Then he had suddenly
realised that an aspirin tablet was, roughly, of the same
size and that the colour could surely be added. It had
taken him hours of patient experiment, but eventually he
produced a bogus tablet. He put it in the bottle in her
handbag.

Of course, he had not believed in success, consequently
his conscience never troubled him. Not, that was, until
Evadne failed to arrive at Charing Cross. . . .

How did a man live with himself when he believed he
was responsible for his wife's death? How did he live,
torn between the mental mælstrom of terror at the
thought of being caught out and the sick desire to be
caught out so that he could be punished and thus expiate
the sin?

He had been bewildered by Stymie's death because that
made nonsense of everything, but he had been too sick
in mind really to try to understand it.

But Evadne had not taken the tablet. Even had she
done so, it would almost certainly not have caused her
death. Perhaps a moralist would still condemn, but for
him the need for expiation had vanished.

Quite suddenly, there came to him the memory of
Jaeger as he said: "By the way, Mr. Leithan, I'd throw
that bottle of tablets away, if I were you—it's never safe
to keep old medicine about the place." Why should
the detective have said such a thing? Had his "tidy"
mind puzzled out all of the truth? Had he searched
through the tablets and found the forgery?

: :   : :

Leithan ran from his car to the front door of Hideaway
House.

When she opened the door and looked at him, Pamela

did so with a wary, nervous, and half-defiant expression. He went inside and closed the door. "They've found her."

She momentarily closed her eyes.

"The reeds were holding her under the lake in Roman Woods. She died from a coronary."

Very slowly, she relaxed. She realised that for her, also, a private nightmare had ended.

THE END